Judge's Official Copy

**The Kiriyama Pacific Rim
Book Prize Entry**

Entry number: _____ *19* _____
Date received: _____ *4/18/97* _____
Date mailed: _____

The Fruit 'N Food

a
novel
by

Leonard Chang

Black Heron Press
Post Office Box 95676
Seattle, Washington 98145

The Fruit 'N Food has been awarded the 1996 Black Heron Press Award for Social Fiction.

ISBN 0-930773-45-4

Published by
  Black Heron Press
  Post Office Box 95676
  Seattle, Washington 98145

For my parents,
Umee Chang Pepe and C. Yul Chang

I would like to thank the following people for their help with various aspects of this book: Renee Cho, Jerry Gold, Judith Grossman, Tom Keneally, Gaby Schwab, and my friends from UCI. A special thanks to Cara, for everything.

ONE

       For six months Tom lay in a hospital bed, blind, in a coma, though he didn't know that—all he knew was that he sometimes heard voices around him, wavering, echoing away, and he couldn't see, couldn't speak. He lived like this until one day someone asked him again to move his hand and he was able to. There was a commotion but he became tired, too tired to do any more tricks, and drifted off. Now, he is just confused.

       We begin this story at the end, to let you know that there is an end, to show you what will come. Perhaps this strategy stems from Tom's inability to view destinations now as he approaches them, his incapacity to see the top of unfamiliar steps, to guide himself towards the door. It is strange being blind. If he doesn't have a voice behind him saying, "About two more feet to your left, Tom," or "There are twelve steps," he gropes forward waiting for that end to come but never being sure if he'll stumble, if he'll begin to lift his foot for another step but land on nothing, if he'll miss the door and have to follow the wall the other way.

The end: After some uncertainty he is alive, unseeing, his face scarred but bandaged. Tom is in the rehabilitation ward of St. Mary's Medical Intensive Care unit. He hasn't spoken yet even though he is physically capable—he is still unsure what is going on—and he wonders if what the doctors say is true, that he will never see again, and if, someday, he will have to use a cane, a guide dog, even learn Braille. Reading by touching terrifies him, though he doesn't know why. He is strangely calm.

It is true when blinded people say that their other senses become more acute. What is even more interesting is that Tom's memory is suddenly embroidered with his other senses, a retroactive filling-in of sound, smell, taste and touch. He can still "see" images in his mind, but they are layered with darkness, and seem to be more so with every passing day. For example, if he were sighted and were to describe the fruit stand at the Korean grocery where he worked, where all this began, the stand which he stared at that first day he saw the store, he would tell you about the apples, oranges and grapefruits separated by a green plastic mesh that snaked around the fruit and hung over the sides; the signs above the apples were newly drawn—white cardboard with black magic marker: Red Delicious, Granny Smith, and MacIntosh apples for sale. The apples were in staggered rows, the hot afternoon sun shining off them at identical angles, the reds and greens contrasting sharply against the bright Sunkist oranges.

But now he senses more: the heavy odor of rotting fruit coming from the side of the store, where the dumpster was. A sweet, citrus smell rises from the fruits, and though he can count the uneven rows right now in his head, marvel at this geometry of fruit, he can also taste the grapefruit that he will soon eat, the tart juiciness filling his mouth, wincing sharpness easing his thirst. At that time, almost a year ago, he looked through the large front window, and saw an Asian man at the counter, ringing up a customer. Tom was there at the store to ask about a job. For the past week he had been looking for work, having just arrived in Kasdan, Queens after losing his job as a waiter in a restaurant in Boston. He spent his childhood in Kasdan, and returned to it since he wanted to live somewhere familiar.

When Tom walked into the Fruit 'N Food grocery for the first time, he was hit by the cool air in the store, the air-conditioner whirring loudly above him. More smells of old fruits and vegetables. A hint of ammonia. The man at the counter turned when the small bell on the door rang; he smiled and nodded slowly at Tom, the tough dry skin wrinkling around his eyes and mouth. The man wore baggy jeans and a loose blue workshirt.

Since the man had a customer, Tom walked further in and pretended to be a shopper. The grocery was small, with only four aisles; the aisle to the far left was filled with more fruit and vegetables, pale heads of cabbages, leafy celery stalks, carrots. The back aisle was refrigerated, and he saw eggs, milk, and further along, beer and soft drinks. A fluorescent bulb in the far right corner flickered rapidly, and beyond the corner in a back room, a woman's voice, an older harsh voice, was scolding someone. A younger female voice answered. Tom recognized the Korean inflections, though he couldn't understand them. He hadn't heard this language in many, many years.

Tom walked to the counter, and the man said something to him in Korean. A question.

"I don't speak Korean," he said.

"You Korean, *hanguk-saddem?*"

Tom nodded.

The man said something again in Korean.

He shook his head.

Laughing quietly, the man also shook his head. "Ho, you no Korean. You *gyupo.*"

Tom hesitated, then said, "I want to buy a grapefruit." He motioned outside. "A pink grapefruit."

"Grapefruit? Three for a dollar."

"I just want one." He reached into his back pocket, but his wallet was gone. He patted his other pockets, cursing to himself.

"What? What wrong?" the man asked.

What was wrong was that he had lost his wallet. As Tom hurried back outside to search the hot concrete, looking under the stand, in the gutter, he began to panic. Had he left it in his apartment? Maybe somewhere along the street? Fifty bucks. His last fifty bucks.

The man walked outside, his short, bulky body moving quickly. "You lose wallet?"

"I think so," Tom told him. "I had all my money in it."

"Maybe it here. We can look," the man said, squatting down slowly, grunting. He squinted and scanned the sidewalk.

After paying the deposit for the apartment, and buying groceries, Tom had given up over two hundred dollars the past two weeks. He tried to remember if he had taken out his wallet any time today.

"It might be around," the man said. He paused, then offered his hand. "My name is Mr. Rhee."

"Thomas. Thomas Pak." They shook hands. Mr. Rhee's grip was strong, and Tom felt the callouses scratch his palm. They continued looking around the sidewalk.

Mr. Rhee stood up slowly, his knees cracking. "I don't see. Maybe you drop somewhere else. Where you live, down there? You hurry or someone take it."

"Yeah," Tom said, looking down Amber Avenue and tiring at the thought of having to search the streets. In fact he was tired, very tired, since he hadn't slept well for the past few nights. Maybe it was the new apartment, or the heat, but he couldn't seem to fall asleep until it was almost light out, and then he woke up at the slightest noise on the street.

"Here," Mr. Rhee said, holding out a clear plastic bag filled with three grapefruits.

Tom hesitated.

"Here, you take. You pay another time."

"I might not find it. I might not have any money."

"It's okay. You take," he said. "You so skinny. You need to eat, get muscle."

Tom thanked him as he grabbed the bag and promised to repay him. Asking him for a job now seemed out of place, especially after receiving this gift. Mr. Rhee shoved his hands into his pockets and said, "You look for wallet now." He returned into the store. Tom wanted to stop him, but kept quiet. Mr. Rhee and the Fruit 'N Food could wait.

He then did what anyone else would have done. He retraced his steps. As he weighed the heavy plastic bag of grapefruit in his hand, he began walking slowly down the street, searching the sidewalks. Amber Avenue, a busy four-laner that runs off the Grand Central Parkway, has on it small stores with iron grilling welded over the windows, garbage piled up on the street waiting for the next pick-up, and a few newspaper stands spread out every three or four blocks. Tom passed and checked the stores he had been in earlier: the row of clothing and shoe stores off Inman, the large pizzeria near Gillan with what looked like new red tables and a smell of pepperoni floating into the street, the camera-electronic store with dozens of equipment stacked in the window. The traffic to his right became more congested as the afternoon approached rush hour, cars honking and cutting each other off, racing home, and he began to hurry down the street, worrying about his money.

Δ

When Tom thinks back about himself, he realizes that that person isn't him. The Tom Pak he sees rushing down Amber Avenue for his lost wallet is so removed from who and what he is now that he barely recognizes him. And yet, those experiences and memories are his, the body, now damaged, is his. Perhaps this is because during those months at the

Fruit 'N Food he wasn't sleeping; he was constantly worried about money and finding a job; he was almost crazy with indirection. He wanted to get settled right away.

After the restaurant in Boston laid off a number of workers, he couldn't seem to find more work. Sure, there were minimum wage jobs in fast-food places that he could have taken, and, in fact, he worked at one fried chicken place for a week. But he soon quit. He couldn't stand the low pay, the uniforms, and the fact that he was the oldest cashier in the place. He was surrounded by high school kids. That was why he decided to move somewhere different.

However, while he searched for his wallet in his apartment that afternoon he was regretting his decision. There wasn't much of an apartment to search through since all he had was an air mattress, a coffee table, and a portable black and white TV that he had brought with him from Boston. His clothes were still strewn around his duffle bags, and it took one quick look to know that the wallet wasn't here. Perhaps he had been pickpocketed. He realized that he had no money, no income, and no idea, really, what to do next. He had some food in the refrigerator, and now he had three grapefruits. Without his wallet he had no identification. He had no identity. Maybe now, he thought as he looked outside his window, eight floors down, the cars jammed as a truck unloaded some boxes in front of a garage—maybe now without his wallet he didn't exist.

Δ

The next morning Tom woke up when a car alarm went off somewhere down the street, and he knew instantly where he had to go this morning. The grocery. He checked his watch and was surprised to learn that it was only seven o'clock. The last time he had checked it had been four a.m. Although he felt tired, and his limbs, particularly his legs, felt oddly heavy this morning, he didn't feel like he had had only a few hours of sleep a night for the past four nights. He felt lightheaded, calm, almost detached, and this was a pleasant feeling. Maybe he could sleepwalk through life and not mind.

He rolled off the mattress and lay on the cool wooden floor, staring up at the paint peeling off the high ceiling. His stomach rumbled. Pressing his hands against his midsection, he felt his ribs and remembered what Mr. Rhee had said yesterday, that he was too skinny. He was. He had to eat more, and maybe if he worked at the grocery he'd get free food. Tom sat up, and became slightly dizzy, so he reached out with his arms that felt much longer than usual and steadied himself. What was happening to him?

He blinked, suddenly remembering a fragment of a dream. Something frightening. He remembered a bright, white light shining into his eyes, hurting him. And it'd been so familiar. Had he dreamt that before?

He showered and shaved, then dressed in jeans and a button-up striped shirt, wanting to look presentable to the Rhees. He checked himself in the mirror and thought he looked like a young Asian Christ, with his gaunt face and deep set eyes. His long hair. He tied a ponytail in back. He ate a grapefruit for breakfast.

Δ

"Here?" Mr. Rhee asked. "You work here?"

Tom nodded. "I've worked in a convenience store before, like this place except no fruit."

Mr. Rhee nodded slowly. "But, hard work here. Many hours. Not like it much."

"I can do it. I need the money."

Studying Tom, Mr. Rhee held up a finger and said, "*Jhankaman.*" He walked to the back room and Tom heard him talking with his wife, their voices low and quiet. He glanced at the counter with the cardboard display of key rings and plastic change purses, the candy jar filled with 5¢ Bazooka gums he remembered buying as a kid, reading the Bazooka Joe comics that came wrapped with the gum; jaw breakers in red, green, blue, and yellow in a smaller candy jar; Skoal chewing tobacco tins stacked neatly on top of one another, the sharp tobacco smell spreading across the counter. I can work here, he thought. I can do this.

After a few minutes Mr. and Mrs. Rhee came out. Mrs. Rhee was also short and compact, like her husband, and her hair was tied into a tight bun, her jeans brand new with the cuffs rolled up, a band of white against the dark blue fabric. She looked Tom over and clucked her tongue when she saw his hair.

"How old are you?" she asked.

"Twenty-six."

"You go to college?"

He shook his head. "I went for a year but dropped out. I'll probably go back someday."

"What do your parents do?"

"My mother died when I was young. My father died when I was in school."

They nodded their heads. They asked him a few more questions about where he was living and what kind of work he had done.

"Okay, try for a few weeks," Mrs. Rhee said. "Then we see. Jung-Me go to summer school, so we use you. You work hard, then we see."

Mr. Rhee said, "Soon we try to open another store in New Jersey. I will be gone more. So maybe we need help."

"We pay," Mrs. Rhee said, "four dollar."

"Isn't that below minimum wage?" Tom

asked.

"Yes," she said.

He paused. "Oh."

Mr. Rhee said, "But we pay cash, off books. No tax."

"Ah."

"And after you work here long, we give more," Mrs. Rhee said.

"Okay. I'll take it," Tom said. "When do I start?"

The Rhees glanced at each other. Mr. Rhee said, "Now?"

"Oh, of course." Tom nodded. "What do you want me to do?"

"I show you things," Mrs. Rhee said, motioning for him to follow. Mr. Rhee went back to the register.

I got the job, Tom thought, dazed. He walked with Mrs. Rhee to the back room, looking over the top of her head, noticing some silver hairs caught in her thick black bun.

Δ

Tom and his father were never very close, and when his father died almost eight years ago, Tom didn't even attend his funeral. He regrets that now, since it was really just his adolescent hatred of his father that turned Tom away, though he realizes that his father tried his best. Without Tom's mother, his father didn't know what to do with him. After Tom's mother died slowly of cancer, his father sent him away first to an aunt in California, then to his grandmother in Korea. Tom spent almost three years being shuttled from relative to relative, until finally his father sent for him and they lived like strangers. Tom can't really complain since he was fed and clothed and was encouraged to read and write, to excel in school, though now he realizes that they never spoke about his mother, never spoke about anything except the most innocent and mundane things. By high school Tom rarely saw him, spending days away with friends, coming home only to ask him for money. And in college, Tom used to open the letters from him and look first to see if there was a check. If not, he threw the letter in a pile, unread, and waited for another. Tom regretted his selfishness once his father died, and he knows now that part of the attraction of the Fruit 'N Food was some inexplicable link to his past.

Δ

That first day at the grocery he learned about the Rhee's rigorous schedule: they arrived there from Riverdale by five in the morning to meet the truck that delivered the new shipment of fruits and vegetables; they set up, and then ran the store all day until they closed at ten, though they didn't leave Kasdan until near midnight. Tom couldn't believe how much work they put into the store, especially considering that they only cleared about thirty thousand total last year, according to Mr. Rhee.

Mrs. Rhee had been impressed with Tom's knowledge of cash registers, alarms, and refrigeration units, so Tom felt at ease with this job. It really wasn't much different from when he had worked at J.J.'s Superette in Boston, before the restaurant job, though J.J.'s had been much simpler. There, during the graveyard shift, he had just watched the TV at the counter and read magazines.

Now, Tom's task at the moment was to re-price the canned vegetables. He was actually marking up the prices by a few cents with the label gun, and had to be careful to stamp the label directly over the old one, so there would be no confusion as to the current price. He had a clipboard with the new prices for each can, referenced by brand, size, and UPC code. Although he had been stamping for the past hour, his hand hurting, with still two shelves left, he found something soothing in the rhythm of the stamping, the clicking in his hand, the small orange labels spitting onto the can and the long thin strip of wax paper extending and curling around his arm. He lined up all the cans and began hitting them with the label gun row by row so that all he had to concentrate on was hitting the old label: Campbell's French Onion with Beef Stock: .99. Cream of Chicken: .66. Tomato Rice: .75. Vegetable: .69. Vegetable Beef: .83. Vegetarian Vegetable: .75. It became a game for him, a test of his aim and concentration, and when he finally finished, he was a little disappointed.

In the back room, which was really a dank concrete windowless cell with boxes of food (canned vegetables, cereals, spaghetti sauce), storage freezers, and a tub of water, Tom then helped Mr. Rhee rearrange some of the heavier boxes and stack them in the corner. Tom grunted when they raised the box and dropped it on the stack. They fell silent as they pushed the surrounding crates away from the center of the floor and when they had finished that, Mr. Rhee motioned to a crate that was used as a desk, a small lamp next to a pot simmering on a hot plate. "Have some *guksoo*," Mr. Rhee said. "You need to eat."

Tom hesitated, but when Mr. Rhee lifted the cover he saw what was in there. "Oh, noodles. Yeah, I'd like that."

"*Guksoo*, not noodles. *Guksoo1*," he said. He poured some of it into a small bowl and handed it to Tom with chopsticks, but paused and also gave him a fork. He called his wife, and said something in Korean. She answered back and joined them. They sat on crates, slurping their lunch. In the dim room lit by two bare hanging bulbs and the lamp on the crate, Tom watched the Rhees from the corner of his eyes, two short bulky figures sitting across from him, intent on their bowls. This seemed unreal to Tom, that he would be here, now, when only two weeks ago he was wandering the streets of Boston, having just been let go and wondering what he would do next.

Mrs. Rhee said, "Another thing I forgot: you watch customers. Many stealings."

Tom looked up.

Mr. Rhee said, "In past three months, we lose almost hundred dollars because of stealings."

"Stealings?"

"They put in coat, in pockets, in bags."

"Shoplifters."

They both nodded. Mrs. Rhee pointed outside. "There is red-button on floor you press," she made a stepping motion, "to call police."

"For hold-up," Mr. Rhee said.

"You've been held up before?"

Mrs. Rhee scowled, and held up four fingers. "Four time," she said. "You watch for *gumdngee.*"

"What? What's that?"

Mr. Rhee said something to his wife in Korean, but she shrugged. She said to Tom, *"Mawla? Gumdngee,* black person." She waved at her face.

"Don't say *gumdngee,*" Mr. Rhee said, shaking his head. He turned to Mrs. Rhee and something else in Korean.

She answered back sharply.

Mr. Rhee sighed and glanced at Tom. *"Gumdngee* is bad word, like nig...nigger."

"What do you mean, watch for them?" Tom asked her, thinking, She's racist. I'm working for a racist?

"Watch? Be careful. They steal, hold-up. They drug man. *Gang-peh,* gangs."

"How did they hold you up?"

Mr. Rhee said, "At night, before closing."

"All of them?"

Mr. Rhee nodded again. "Very scared. A gun, screaming 'Ah ya gimme money gimme money!' at me, man shaking from drugs." He demonstrated with his hand jerking back and forth. Then he made a pistol with his fingers. "I don't know what happen to me. Bang, I dead. Very scared."

"The police?"

He smiled sadly, shrugging. He lifted his chopsticks out of his bowl for an instant. "Come too late always. And never find robber. Never."

Mrs. Rhee clucked her tongue. Then, the bell rang outside and she stood up quickly, handing her bowl to her husband. She hurried out.

"What about a gun," Tom said. He thought about his working here, and what if something like that happened to *him*? "Don't you have one, in case?"

Mr. Rhee said, "We have small pistol, but hide under counter and never use."

"But why?"

"More dangerous. Robber could kill," he said.

Tom thought about this. He shook his head. "Why do you do this then? Why not something else, something safer?"

Mr. Rhee laughed to himself, looking at Tom and smiling very slowly. He waved his chopsticks around, two wooden pointers dripping noodle soup. "I don't like this," he said. "But we have nothing." He laughed quietly again. They heard Mrs. Rhee ringing up the customers, the electronic beeps of the register the only sound coming from the other room. Mr. Rhee laughed quietly again. He looked around the small cell. "This is everything."

TWO

In the hospital Tom spends most of the
time in the bed sleeping. Even his waking hours are
spent in a groggy, apathetic state, and though he
listens to those around him, to the TV on his far left,
and even sometimes nods to a question if he feels like
it, he seems to be in a trance. Part of it might be the
painkillers the nurses are giving him. When the
pounding in his head becomes too loud and throbbing, he struggles back and forth until someone comes
by and pushes some pills into his mouth, bringing his
hand up to touch a cool glass of water. Sometimes
they don't come for a long time, and he wishes he
could rip off his bandages and grab the pain, but if he
even touches his bandages, the fire in his head wors-
ens. After he takes the pills, everything around him
dulls, the pain subsides, and he sleeps. He loses all
sense of time.

Compare this state with how he was
during those months in Kasdan. There, he couldn't

seem to sleep for more than a few hours a night. Even after his first few days at the grocery in which he worked himself close to exhaustion, he'd end up lying awake on his mattress, listening to the traffic sounds outside—a noisy car driving by, honking, different alarms—and he'd stare at the moonlit shadows along his wall. He had to be at the grocery by seven in the morning, and on that particular evening, his fifteenth day in the apartment, his third night at the Fruit 'N Food, he checked his watch again and saw that it was three-thirty a.m.

He couldn't believe he had been lying there for that long. Tom sat up and leaned against the wall, rolling his neck back and forth. His apartment looked like it was underwater—dark, murky, and suffused with a dim, blue moonlight, and despite the distress this lack of sleep caused him, he liked the peacefulness of the late evening. He was getting used to this: a slow-motion dance of sounds and lights in this soup, and often he would then turn on his portable TV and the screen would burst into the room, sending flickering shadows around him, the voices on low, and he would become hypnotized by the glow in front of him.

Tonight he did not watch TV. Instead, Tom stood up slowly and lifted his arms, testing the waters, and stretched his back which was hurting from the mattress. He swam towards the window and looked out. Kasdan in the late night. The cracked and dirty sidewalks were transformed in the darkness—shimmering streets from a light rain reflected the soft white street lamps, the moon, and he thought, This isn't real. I'm not real.

Exhaustion softened his vision, and he opened the window slightly to let in some air. A cool draft blew onto his naked body. He felt a faint humming in his arms and legs, a whirring of protest at still having to move after almost ten hours of work today. And his mind still hadn't calmed down, the prices of the canned soups and vegetables still passing through his head. He had unintentionally memorized the prices.

Gliding back to his mattress he eased himself back down and sank deeper into the tangled sheets. He had a job. That was good. No matter what had happened before, and what would happen next, he had found himself a place he liked, and a source of pay. It seemed to be working out, this job, since he was not only getting a feel for what he needed to do, but the Rhees were getting used to him. He wasn't sure if he liked Mrs. Rhee, and sometimes she hounded him too much about his work, but he'd have to see. Tomorrow he had to be there at seven, and this reminder forced him to relax his body and he prayed for sleep again. He closed his eyes.

Δ

When he arrived Mrs. Rhee frowned at him. "You are late," she said to him.

Mr. Rhee, who came out with a basket of washed fruit to put on the stand, said to his wife, "We make him come very early. A few minutes is okay."

"We pay him so he should come."

Tom cleared his throat. "Sorry." According to his watch he wasn't late, and for the past two days he had been early, but he let it go. Tomorrow he'd be here earlier. He hurried into the back room to get an apron.

"Today," Mr. Rhee said when Tom came out to help him. "Today after set-up you take register."

Tom thought, Finally. It seemed to him the easiest job here, sitting behind the counter and ringing up purchases.

He and Mr. Rhee began placing the fruit in the wooden stand out front, being careful not to bruise anything. It was a cool morning, though by ten the streets would be warming up and by noon they would have to keep the door closed and the air-conditioner on high. Tom glanced up and down Jenkins; he looked over the corner towards Amber. It was probably best that this store wasn't directly on Amber, otherwise the traffic and dirt might make the store unappealing, but here on Jenkins, it wasn't as busy, and sometimes when he sat out here to watch the stand, he liked looking across the street at the "Checks Cashed" store with the green neon dollar signs buzzing in the small, prison-like windows, and the newspaper stand at the opposite corner that also sold small jewelry; a black velvet board stood next to the newspapers, clusters of fake necklaces and earrings hanging from small tacks. Right now a truck was backing into a warehouse a block down, beeping loudly into the street.

"Tomorrow, on weekends, Jung-Me will come to help," Mr. Rhee said.

"Your daughter?"

He nodded. "She has summer school right now, but in afternoon tomorrow I want to go to New Jersey to look for locations."

Locations, Tom thought. Expansion was on their minds. They always seemed to be moving forward. "What do you look for in locations?" he asked. He finished with the apples and moved to the oranges. His stomach grumbled.

"If other grocery nearby, if many *hanguk-saddem.*" He paused. "Korean people."

A thin sticky film from the oranges collected on Tom's hands. He wiped it on his apron.

Mr. Rhee continued. "If the *keh* gives the money, and if this store does good, then we expand." Then, almost to himself he added, "We have to think about Jung-Me's college money."

Tom concentrated on the fruits, half-listening, placing oranges two at a time into the stand.

After they finished loading the fruit and hanging the small portable scale from the low bar supporting the awning, Tom went inside and took over the register for Mrs. Rhee. She tested him on it again, for the third time, asking him to ring up certain things, then void it, which he did. It was a small Sharp electronic register with a flat touch keyboard, the digital numbers lighting up green on the black display, and this was connected to a small electronic scale that was activated whenever something was placed on it. There was a small key on the register, turned to the "Sale" notch. Tom surveyed the area behind the counter and saw the red button on the floor underneath the lowest shelf.

"The alarm," Tom said.

Mrs. Rhee said it was, and demonstrated using it by making a stepping motion.

"How fast does it work?"

"Not fast. Very slow," she said. She moved agilely from behind the counter, despite her bulk. Tom realized he had never seen the daughter and tried to imagine an offspring of the Rhees. "If you need help, call me," Mrs. Rhee said. "I be out here."

Settling into the chair, Tom examined the things back here: plastic and paper bags for the customers' purchases, the rack of cigarettes above him, the cartons behind him, a green Lotto machine to his left, a drawer with scratch-off lottery tickets, a pile of rags, a small box filled with pencils and pens. He saw a small radio next to the Lotto machine and turned it on. He found a news station, liking the sounds of crackling voices around him.

The morning passed slowly, with only a few men coming in to buy some beer, and they had looked strung out, the harried, bloodshot eyes, the slow gait. A news story came on the radio about the continuing boycott of a Korean grocery in Brooklyn's Flatbush section after a Haitian woman accused the owners of assaulting her. Tom had heard about this while he had been in Boston, though he hadn't paid much attention. He turned up the volume and listened to an editorial about the racist legacy of New York: Willie Turks, a black transit worker killed by a mob of whites yelling racist slurs; Bernhard Goetz; Howard Beach; the Central Park rape. The editorial urged for more communication, more dialogue.

An elderly woman came in and he turned down the radio. Tom suddenly wondered about this store, this neighborhood, and wanted to know if he could be in any danger. He had never worried about this before.

Mr. Rhee came out of the back room with some garbage. Tom stopped him. "What's all this I'm hearing about the boycott and race problems?" he asked. "Are there problems here?" He remembered Mrs. Rhee's comments that first day.

"Some problem," Mr. Rhee said, putting the plastic bag down. Clinking glass.

"Like what?"

"Stealings, robberies."

"Like Brooklyn?"

Mr. Rhee's face tightened. "No no. Not like Brooklyn. We have good relation." He picked up the garbage. "No problems like Brooklyn."

"So we don't have to worry about that kind of thing?"

Mr. Rhee nodded and carried the bag outside.

Tom watched his broad back disappear around the doorway. The elderly woman, wearing matching dark orange plaid blouse and pants, approached the counter with a loaf of bread and a bag of tomatoes in her basket. He smelled her hair spray, a medicinal flowery smell that he didn't like. He rang her up, and handed her the change. Her small, withered hands spotted with age shook slightly as she counted the coins and slipped them into her purse. She smiled when Tom told her to have a nice day.

As she walked slowly out of the store, Tom heard Mrs. Rhee say hello to her. He then thought about the robberies and remembered the gun that was supposed to be under the counter. Making sure the Rhees weren't watching, he bent down and searched for it. There. Behind the rags. He didn't know anything about guns and stared at it for a second, not getting too close to it. He thought it might be one of those Saturday Night Specials he had seen on the news, but he wasn't sure, and he didn't want to touch it, didn't want to disturb it. He pushed the rags back, and sat in the chair. There was something menacing about having a gun within his reach, and he felt vaguely uncomfortable. He tried not to think about it, and when the noon rush of customers began, he stood and worked quickly at the register. He was careful, though, to watch the customers in the mirrors—two concave mirrors in the opposite corner warping images and distances, and a third one, long and rectangular, angled along the rear so he could see the back aisle—to watch for stealings.

Δ

Before Tom left for the evening, Mrs. Rhee paid him his wages for the week—payday would be Fridays, she told him as she rang open the register and counted out one hundred and thirty-six dollars, checking the small piece of paper with Tom's daily hours listed, hours which hadn't been consistent this week because the Rhees hadn't needed him the full day on Tuesday and Wednesday. Tom accepted the money and thanked her.

Money! He felt the small wad of bills in his pocket and he noticed as he walked home that he was suddenly lighter, freer, and he knew he had been really worried about money even though he wouldn't let himself think about it. He was okay for now. He could treat himself to dinner. He paused at the electronics store, still open, and stared at the equipment. He could buy a radio. But he continued on.

At the pizza parlor with the new red tables and the pepperoni smell that drifted out into the street, Tom couldn't resist buying a slice and a soda. He sat by the window and watched the traffic on Amber, some people jaywalking and weaving around cars that had stopped moving to let a truck pull out. He saw a group of young boys walking on the opposite side of the street dribbling a basketball and passing it to each other, dodging a trickling stream of people moving towards them. In the pizza parlor, there were a few teenagers at one table by the rear wall, and an elderly black woman leafing through a newspaper a few tables from Tom.

The door opened and four black men walked in. The customers, Tom included, looked up for a second, then went back to their food, but Tom watched them move towards the counter, two of them talking loudly, and order a pizza. One man, wearing a nylon jacket with "Kung Fu" embroidered on the back, looked around and stared at Tom for a second. Tom tensed, thinking about that editorial and wondering if this neighborhood had racial problems. It never had when he had been living here, but this wasn't the same place. Then he thought he was being stupid, worrying and making assumptions for no real reason. And he realized that had he not heard the editorial, he wouldn't have thought about all this. He was being too sensitive.

He took another bite of his pizza, the garlic and spicy pepperoni burning his tongue, and listened to the men talk about a car one of them was buying. What was he worried about? They didn't care about him. No one did. First Mrs. Rhee, then the editorial, and now he was getting jumpy about the stupidest things. Just forget it.

Tom inhaled the warm, greasy smell of pizza and thought that there wasn't anything better than this right now. He felt a dull ache in the back of his neck, and his body was heavy from exhaustion, but damn, this pizza was good.

THREE

Though he made it to the grocery early, he still hadn't had more than a few hours of sleep the night before, and he could feel it beginning to affect him. It seemed as if everything was louder, brighter, even smelled stronger. Perhaps this is his memory embellishing his senses, but no, he distinctly remembers walking into the Fruit 'N Food that morning and being hit not only by the familiar blast of cool air, but by a suffocating stench of old vegetables. He became nauseous and had to keep still. He squinted at the lights. After a few seconds he recovered and said hello to Mrs. Rhee, who watched him carefully and then asked if he was all right. He said he was.

Mrs. Rhee's daughter, upon hearing them, poked her head out from the back room. She stepped out and said hello. She was short, coming up to Tom's chest, and slightly overweight with full cheeks. Her long black hair was shiny under the bright lights, and even from across the store Tom thought he could smell a faint scent of perfume. She smiled. "You must be Thomas."

"Yes. Jung-Me?"

"Actually I prefer 'June'," she said. She pushed some of her hair off her shoulder and straightened her grey NYU T-shirt.

Mrs. Rhee said to Tom, "Mr. Rhee will be back at lunch. You finish setting up stand outside."

Tom nodded to June and walked back outside, the heat prickling his skin. He saw the crate of apples and oranges next to the empty stand, and pulled the plastic cover off, lining the stand with the green mesh. He began loading the fruit. He thought June had inherited her parents' stockiness, a big-boned, strong body, and he wondered what was it like to be stocky and strong, instead of tall and gangly like him. He often felt clumsy, his feet too big, his limbs too long, and even doing something like this, stacking fruit, became more difficult since he had to stoop over and his lower back would begin to hurt.

June came out with a smaller crate of grapefruit. "My mom says to leave some room for these." She placed it next to him and Tom couldn't help noticing that she wasn't wearing a bra; her breasts pressed against her shirt, and he saw the slight bumps of her nipples. He looked away, embarrassed, and continued adding the apples two by two onto the stand.

"Oh, I need my apron," he said, and walked back inside, confused by his flushed face. He hoped she hadn't seen him staring. But with her at the store, he felt something different, and he wasn't sure if it was just the fact that he hadn't had sex for so long, or if he might be attracted to her. The last time he had had sex had been with one of the waitresses at the restaurant in Boston. He had just started working there, and a woman working her way through college, Laurie Ferrar, became friendly with him. They went out a few times, but after a month or so, she took a better paying job across town, and they soon lost interest in each other. Tom suddenly realized that he was becoming excited at the thought of her. Though they had little in common, and tended to get drunk whenever they were together, they loved touching each other in bed, stroking each other's body.

When he returned outside, June was playing with the hanging scale, pushing and pulling the pan, testing the weights. She then leaned back against the door, her hands behind her back, her legs crossed, and watched him tie on his apron.

She asked, "So you grew up here?"

He nodded. "But I haven't been back for a while."

She began helping him load the oranges. "Where were you?"

He told her.

June took this in and said, "I might want to go to college up there."

Tom felt his arms tiring, so he slowed his pace. He really didn't feel like talking right now, since it was too early and he was having trouble thinking clearly. Her perfume was much stronger now, a strawberry hint to it. "That's great," he said without much enthusiasm. He saw some of her long shiny hair brush over the oranges, the contrast in color and texture odd to him. "What grade are you in?" he asked.

"Twelfth this fall. My last."

So young, he thought. Too young. He nodded and finished the oranges, moving onto the grapefruits.

"You have no...relatives around?" she asked.

He paused. "No. I have an aunt in California, though I'm not sure if she's still there."

She stared at him, and this made him uncomfortable. He pretended to arrange some grapefruit.

"So you're all alone out here?"

He nodded.

"Wow. Must be nice."

This surprised him. He turned to her and said, "You think so?"

Δ

By the early afternoon Tom was at the register listening to a classical radio station because anything else seemed too harsh for his ears. The store had just emptied and he was glad to have a chance to sit back in the small plastic chair and close his eyes. Mrs. Rhee was outside, watching the fruit, and June was in the back room. He liked the quiet. Though, as soon as he relaxed, June came out and took a can of soda from the refrigerated aisle. She approached him, opening the can.

"What did you study when you were in college?" she asked. He had mentioned his one year to her.

Tom sighed inwardly. He knew she meant well, but he just didn't feel like talking right now. "Math. I liked Math."

Then, a tall black man with long dreadlocks walked in, the bell ringing as he pushed open the door and paused for a second. He flipped his dreadlocks behind his head and took his hands out of his green army jacket. Mrs. Rhee stood behind the glass door, watching him. She sometimes did this and it unnerved Tom, making *him* watch whomever it was—usually a young black man or woman—nervously, almost expecting something to happen.

"What kind of math?"

He turned towards her. "What?"

"What kind of math did you like?"

"Geometry. Theory."

The man inspected the snack foods, his hollowed, weathered face moving closer to the shelf, his hair falling across his stubbled cheek. His jacket hung open and Tom hoped the man wouldn't shoplift. By the way the jacket was opened, it'd be easy to slip something inside, and then Tom wouldn't know what to do. The man straightened up and walked down the other aisle, his steps slow and deliberate.

"I hate math. I'm thinking of pre-law."

Tom glanced at Mrs. Rhee staring and he wished she weren't so obvious—her arms folded across her chest, feet apart, chin jutting forward almost touching the glass, her body motionless. The man seemed not to notice her, and continued to browse the aisles, letting his eyes linger on one item, then another. When the man suddenly turned and approached the front counter, Mrs. Rhee stiffened. Tom wasn't sure if she saw something he hadn't, and he glanced at June, who was drinking her soda, staring off into a corner, thinking. He looked back towards Mrs. Rhee and moved his foot closer to the alarm button.

"Do you know anything about pre-law?"

The man walked slowly, looking from side to side rather than straight ahead, and each step of his heavy black boots squeaked on the linoleum.

When the man reached the counter, he stared directly at Tom, unblinking, and paused. Tom remained calm and told himself he was being stupid and no one would try to rob a store in the middle of the day. Mrs. Rhee was being irrational. He arranged the lottery tickets in the drawer, glancing up at the man, and asked if he could help him.

The man hesitated, then asked for a pack of Pall Malls, and dug into his pocket for money, handing Tom a few crumpled bills. The man's fingers were long and bony, the back of his hands grey with dryness.

Reaching up into the cigarette dispenser and pulling out a hard pack, Tom rung up the purchase and gave the man his change, thanking him. The man nodded. As he moved towards the door, Mrs. Rhee slid out of view.

Goddammit, Tom thought as the door bell went of again and the man left. His heart was beating rapidly. June was saying something.

"...what are some good colleges around here? Tom?"

He turned to her. "Listen, I'm kind of busy right now," he said, more sharply than he had intended.

She blinked and drew back. Then, after a few seconds, she said, "Okay." She walked towards the back room and Tom rubbed his temples. He wanted to stop her and say something more, but couldn't think clearly.

A new wave of customers came in and Tom glanced outside but didn't see Mrs. Rhee. She was making him crazy. Doing that damn thing.... He had to calm down. He looked guiltily towards the back room. He shouldn't have snapped at June. Ah, hell. Why couldn't everyone just leave him alone and let him do his job? His heart still thumped in his chest. He inhaled deeply. When a line formed at the counter he soon lost himself in his work, the electronic beeps of the buttons, the opening and closing of the drawer, will that be all, your change, thank you very much—this went on as he glanced at the purchases, the soaps, potato chips, cigarettes, tampons, candy, coffee, fruits, vegetables, and all these things blurred in front of him as he began moving mechanically, becoming an extension of the register.

Later, when business slowed down, he went into the back room. June was sitting at the crate with both hands clamped on her forehead, leaning forward and reading, the lamp shining brightly onto her open textbook. He leaned against the open door, and cleared his throat. She turned slightly towards him and looked at him with one eye, the other underneath her hands.

"Uh, about before...."

She sat up.

"Sorry about that," he said.

"About what?"

"About snapping at you."

She ran a crooked finger along her temple and pushed some hair behind her ear. "Don't worry about it," she said. "I guess you're still getting used to the job." She then looked at him more closely. "You look really tired."

He nodded. "I haven't been sleeping much. Insomnia."

"Really? You know," she said, searching through her purse. "I have some sleeping pills...." She pulled out a few packets and handed one to Tom.

"You use these?" he asked, reading the label. Sleep-All. Not for resale.

"We get free samples."

"Why do you need sleeping pills?"

"To sleep."

He was about to say something like, Aren't you too young, but checked himself. "Thanks." He turned and looked back into the store. "I should get to work."

"Hey, Tom?"

He put the pills in his pocket and waited.

"I was wondering," she said, flipping some pages in her book. She folded her leg underneath her and sat awkwardly in her chair. "Hey, do you want to go out for a coffee or something?"

Tom hesitated, then said, "Thanks, but I think I need to rest."

She nodded. "Okay. Maybe some other time."

He walked back to the register, not sure what to make of that. She was asking him out, wasn't she?

Δ

That night, Tom, after taking a long, hot shower, studied the two blue sleeping pills in the TV light and rolled them back and forth in his palm. He had never taken drugs to sleep before, and worried about being trapped. He remembered that fragment of a nightmare a few nights ago, and though he didn't think the dream had returned—but how could it with only a few hours of sleep a night?—he didn't like the idea of not being able to wake up if the dream became too much for him. He had had nightmares as a small child, especially after his mother had died, but he had always woken up during or before what he had thought were the worst parts.

Tom swallowed the pills quickly, not allowing himself to change his mind. The tablets seemed to stick in his throat, so he sipped some water from the bathroom faucet, and felt it wash down.

While lying on his mattress and watching the news, Tom knew that he could sleep in tomorrow, since on Sundays the store opened at ten. Tom and Mrs. Rhee had talked today about possibly taking Sundays off beginning next week, since June was around. Although Tom liked the idea, he still needed the money. And it wasn't like he had other things to do.

He sunk into his pillow, gripping it as he began to feel sleepy, unsure if the pills worked this fast, but maybe they did, and he tried to prepare himself for an uncertain journey.

Δ

In a confusing whirlwind of voices, blurring lights as he moved his head around the room, Tom struggled up from the mattress, feeling as if he had been tied down, a commercial jingle blaring at his ears. He groped along the floor for support, knowing that he must get to the bathroom now, bathroom now, and his stomach churned, knotted up, and when he pressed his midsection the pain worsened. He lowered himself back down and cradled himself, waiting for the pain to subside. He felt the sickly sourness in his throat again, the bile and acidic reminders; the gagging beginning. He tried to stand, and the pain sharpened. A cold sweat. The TV began laughing—canned, laugh-trak laughter encircling him—and he coughed and struggled up, trying to hurry to the bathroom, his vision blurry. He fell in front of the toilet and hung over the rim, retching for a second, then threw up, his mouth, his nose, unable to breathe, and when he finally finished he spit and spit but couldn't get the taste out of his mouth, and he was too tired to stand and walk to the sink, so he sat there, listening to the toilet refill itself with the sighing, trickling of water, the cool rim against his cheek. He thought about the sleeping pills and wasn't sure if he had been poisoned or simply had a terrible reaction, but it didn't matter because he was beginning to feel better already and he remembered more of his dream, the blinding light all around him, searing his vision and paralyzing him, and he didn't know why it was so frightening but it was and he shuddered, wanting only to keep still and wait until his nausea completely passed.

Δ

Sunday morning. Tom woke up and felt rested. He wasn't sure if last night had been a dream, but when he saw the bathroom with dried specks of vomit on the toilet he knew it had happened and he was angry at June for giving him those things. But he felt better this morning. Less exhausted than usual.

It was only eight-thirty but he knew he wouldn't be able to go back to sleep, so he showered and dressed, and cleaned the bathroom. By nine he was on his way out—it was sunny and he wanted to take a walk. Except for some cars and a few yellow cabs, the streets were quiet, and he watched the sun rise over the small buildings, and cast long angular shadows over the wide streets. He passed the small delicatessens with some joggers in their neon tights and bright yellow Walkmans clutched in their sweaty hands coming in for a morning juice; the small coffee shops with a few tables out in front beginning to open for the Sunday morning newspaper readers—a waiter setting out small plastic chairs, sweeping the sidewalks. Most of the stores were closed, though, and Tom continued walking, occasionally feeling a bead of water drip down from his wet hair. Yes, the neighborhood had changed: sidewalks crumbling with chunks of curb missing, broken glass and garbage strewn in the gutters, graffiti all along the older buildings on Freemont, the street parallel to Amber.

He remembered when this had been a well-kept, lower-middle-class area, with Italians and small pockets of blacks, Latinos, and Asians. Now, after seeing more of this neighborhood these past few days, Tom saw that everything had become older, more run down, and ethnically it seemed that the majority of residents were black, West Indian, and as he went further north, more Latino. Or maybe he had remembered things wrong, though he distinctly recalled a larger Korean community, especially near Michaelson Park, with a Korean church that his father had attended, and even a few stores next to it with Korean signs and their English translations. But the church wasn't there anymore. Neither were the stores. Instead, these had been torn down and replaced by a three-level parking structure, with a thick chain-link fence on the lower level and indecipherable graffiti decorating the smooth, dirty grey concrete face. A thin layer of grime had descended on Kasdan.

After walking for about a half hour, Tom found himself in front of the Fruit 'N Food. He hadn't realized that he had been heading in this direction, and when he suddenly recognized the empty wooden stand in front, the clear plastic cover tied tightly over them, he looked around and wondered how he had arrived there. All he remembered was wandering between Freemont and Amber, looking in store windows.

"Thomas, you here early?" Mr. Rhee said, opening the front door. He had seen Tom through the large window.

"I was just walking around."

"And you come here?" Mr. Rhee smiled "Want to start early?"

Shaking his head, Tom said, "I was just walking around."

Mr. Rhee continued to grin, and then motioned quickly for Tom to follow him back inside. Tom did. When he walked in he saw Mrs. Rhee at the front counter with a Korean newspaper, staring at him curiously. She asked something to Mr. Rhee in Korean, and Mr. Rhee replied. Mrs. Rhee laughed, her voice harsh, and said to Tom, "You like store, yes?"

Tom nodded and followed Mr. Rhee into the back room. He handed Tom a bowl of noodles with a pair of chopsticks. "*Guksoo*," Tom said.

"Ho, you speak *hanguk* now. Eat. *Muhguh*. Take some fruit too." He made circular eating motions with two fingers to his mouth.

Tom took the bowl and ate some of the steaming noodles. He wasn't hungry, and the spicy beef flavor with the red peppers seemed too strong to have this early in the morning, but he ate it anyway, his eyes watering, his nose running. "Where's June?" he asked as he began sweating on his forehead.

"She come later. She is with friend in Forest Hills. She sleeps over."

Tom had trouble getting all of the noodles with the chopsticks, but when he saw Mr. Rhee drink directly from the bowl, he did the same.

When they finished Mr. Rhee looked up at the clock and said, "We begin now?"

Tom agreed.

By the late morning when everything was set up, Tom helped Mr. Rhee record the new shipments of canned goods in the back room. Tom's eyes were beginning to hurt in the dim light, the numbers on his clipboard becoming fuzzy. Mr. Rhee noticed him squinting, and walked to the crates, turning on the desk lamp and aiming it towards them. They continued to work in silence. Tom tried to ignore the smell of rotting cabbage, and concentrated on the checklist. He was reviewing the number of canned goods from the New Jersey distributor, and Mr. Rhee was checking the invoices from the Queens distributor. The dehumidifier in the corner, a small brown cabinet with slats in the front, clicked on and whirred, drying the damp air.

Then they heard laughter coming from outside, a loud crack on the sidewalk, and curses. Tom looked out the door and saw Mrs. Rhee rushing outside. She began to yell, "You come back you come back!" Tom and Mr. Rhee hurried out and saw the oranges and apples rolling onto the sidewalk and street, and Mrs. Rhee still shouting at two teenagers running away. Mr. Rhee jumped down and stopped the flood of oranges from leaving the broken stand— one wooden leg was jutting awkwardly from under the tilted platform, and had it not been for the plastic mesh most of the oranges would have rolled away. Tom immediately helped Mr. Rhee pick up the fruit and place them with the grapefruits, the mix of colors and textures, apples with grapefruits, jarring. Mrs. Rhee told Mr. Rhee what had happened. She then said to Tom, "They run into stand, break it."

Tom looked up from examining the leg and nodded. He saw that the base—where the holes from the screws had been stripped out by the leverage—could be fixed by simply turning the leg around and making new holes. He told them this. "If you have the tools I can fix this right now."

"Are you sure?" Mr. Rhee asked.

He said he was and Mr. Rhee found the tool box. Tom kneeled on the hard pavement and removed the screws. He wondered if this sort of thing happened often. This didn't seem like the safest place to have this store, especially one which was so accessible with its stand out in front and its wide-open door. He grunted as he tried to tighten the screws into the wood. His hands hurt from the friction of the old screwdriver, from the wooden handle, but after twenty minutes he managed to reconnect the leg. Mr. Rhee, who had been coming out to check on him, inspected the job, was satisfied.

"Mrs. Rhee and me, we think you do good job here," he said.

"Thanks," Tom replied, shrugging and looking at the stand. He smiled to himself.

FOUR

If you ever want to talk, contact me through the nurse, the soft voice tells him. He doesn't say anything as usual, and after a few more minutes of unanswered questions, his counselor says, *I'll come back in a few days. Maybe you'll feel better then. You have physical therapy in about an hour.* Tom lies back down into the cool sheets and listens to the footsteps fade away. She tries very hard to talk with him, but Tom doesn't want to be with anyone. He now has to wait for the man who will come in and lead him into a room smelling of warmth and sweat, where Tom will walk slowly back and forth between two bars, where he will climb shakily up and down stairs that lead nowhere, where he will push against immovable objects. The man knows that this one isn't a talker, but the atrophying muscles are getting the work out they need. This one won't waste away, at least not physically.

In bed, Tom listens to the TV in the background and lets himself drift. He remembers that incident with the broken stand, and wishes he could have done even more for them. But he knows he worked very hard, did his best. After a week had passed at the store, he became used to the lack of sleep and long hours. He was gaining some of his weight back, at least he thought so since his ribs no longer pushed tightly against his skin, and he attributed this to his late-night meals, usually around one in the morning, when he would try to be in bed by eleven hoping for an early night but of course he would end up staring at the ceiling with the peeling paint, long white tongues hanging down at him, and by one o'clock he'd get up and either make himself a sandwich or walk downstairs to the burger place across the street, open until two. He was not worrying so much about money.

While working at the store, he discovered that he hated being a cashier the most, even though he had thought it would be the easiest job. His fingers hurt from pressing the keys and he had to keep an eye on the customers, a task which made the muscles in his back tighten, especially when some of the regulars off the street came in. There was one man, a small skinny junkie who always wore tattered jeans and a ski hat, who had the shakes and yelled often at nothing, at the air around him. Mrs. Rhee knew how to handle him. She'd say, "What you

want? Get what you want and be quiet!" The man
would listen. But Tom couldn't do that, and he felt
his body tightening whenever the man walked in.
There were also a couple of drunks coming in every
morning for a beer to hold them over until the bars
opened. All they wanted was a beer, but Tom couldn't
help tensing up and worrying about what might
happen. They always seemed annoyed at him, especially when he told them how much they owed.

Not all customers were like that, of
course, but he still couldn't relax while working the
register, and on Friday morning when Mrs. Rhee
asked him to leave the register to move more oranges
from the back room to the stand outside, he was
thankful.

Tom grabbed the bottom of the crate, his
fingers scratching the cement floor, and strained his
legs and back, struggling, his neck beginning to sweat.
The wood dug into his forearms, which instead of
hurting actually felt good, since the sharp pain seemed
to wake up his arms. Lowering the crate onto the
pavement outside, he stretched his back and began
adding oranges to cover the bare spots. Oranges had
been selling well, and they had put in an extra order
for next week. The tart smell of fresh citrus was
powerful, making his nose itch.

Tom noticed through the propped open
door two elderly women, both with a box of straw-

berries, speaking loudly to each other about the weather. Their hair was almost identical in style—relaxed, hairsprayed afro with a hairnet, but one had more grey than the other. They wore ankle-length tan and yellow dresses, frumpy white blouses, and their flat shoes tapped the floor in small, quick steps. They placed their strawberries on the counter and Mrs. Rhee began ringing them up.

"That's separate please," one of the ladies said.

Mrs. Rhee sighed, shook her head, and voided the sale. She rang up the first one and said, "Two twenty," bagging the strawberries.

The woman clucked as she handed over three dollar bills, one by one. Mrs. Rhee took the money without looking up and put the change on the counter, next to the bag. The woman nudged the other with her elbow.

Mrs. Rhee rang up the other and said, "Two thirty-five."

"How come mine is more?"

"They price by weight. Hers less so cost less." Mrs. Rhee took the money, still looking at the register. She pushed the change on the counter and bagged the strawberries. The woman slid the change off the counter into her hand. As the two walked out, they whispered to each other. Mrs. Rhee watched them, then went back to wiping the counter.

After Tom had finished, he sat outside on the stool to watch the fruit and positioned himself near the door. He heard the talk radio fading in and out from the magazine stand on the far corner, the smell of garbage and oil coming from Amber, fruit and pine cleaner from the store. There was a laundromat down the street from the Fruit 'N Food, and next to that he saw the photo I.D. store with a big portable yellow sign, "We Make I.D.'s" standing in front.

An hour later, three young teenagers walked past the sign towards Tom; two wearing silky shirts—pea green and white—one wearing grey parachute pants and a black T-shirt. They were talking rapidly and one was laughing. The tall one with a small ponytail glanced at Tom as they walked into the store.

Tom watched an elderly black man in an old brown suit shuffle into the Checks Cashed store. A few minutes later he walked out, hands in his frayed jacket pockets, and he paused to look up in the sky. Tom also looked up but saw nothing, only the blue sky with large grey sweeping clouds.

Then, Mrs. Rhee began yelling inside. "Stop that! I see you! Stop that!" Before Tom had a chance to stand, the three teenagers jumped out of the store, knocking him over, and disappeared around the corner, laughing. Tom sat on the ground, stunned, and after a few seconds realized what had happened and scrambled up. He rushed inside, running into Mrs. Rhee, her shoulders jabbing him in his chest. "Ya!" she cried. She grabbed the door frame for support.

Tom backed up, rubbing his chest. "What'd they do?"

"Why you let them go? Stop them!"

He turned to run after them, but hesitated. He would never catch them now. He shook his head. "They're too far ahead."

"You sit here to stop them! You let them go!"

"They were too fast. I didn't know what—"

"This your job when you sit here. You make sure no one go without pay!" She spat these words. "You don't let no one go without pay!"

"Okay, okay, take it easy. What did they steal?"

"*Aigoo*, no take easy! You—"

Mr. Rhee came out and they began talking in Korean. She pointed at Tom and spoke harshly, but Mr. Rhee calmed her down and sent her back into the store. He looked at Tom. "They just take small things."

"Are you going to call the police?"

He shook his head. "Not worth it. But

next time you try to stop, okay?"

Tom said he'd try, and Mrs. Rhee went back in. What if he had tried to? What then? A fight? Tom shook off the dirt on his pants and sat back on the stool, angry. Mrs. Rhee didn't have to yell at him.

The elderly man crossed the street and approached Tom. "You okay? T-Took a fall," he said. His stutter was very strong, and his voice low, almost a whisper. He scratched his thin, wrinkled face, pausing over his grey stubble. "T-Trouble?" This took a while to come out. Tom felt slightly embarrassed and pretended not to notice.

Tom told him that it was just some kids shoplifting.

"Yeess, these young folk," he said, stuttering less when he spoke slowly. "The city's in trouble."

Tom nodded and watched him wipe his forehead with an unsteady hand. His greying afro was cut close to his scalp.

"The drugs, you know. When my late wife Marian and I—when we moves here twenty years ago...no drugs at all, no sir."

"Twenty years ago?"

"Twenty-four." He nodded. "I ain't seen you here before. Where's the other girl?"

"June?"

"That's right."

"Summer school."

"Yeess." He nodded slowly, thinking, then smiled at Tom. "I's going to check on Mrs. Rhee, if you don't mind."

He walked inside and Tom heard Mrs. Rhee welcome him. "Ya, Mr. Harris, how you do today?" Their voices lowered as they began talking, and Tom continued rubbing his chest, annoyed at himself for not reacting quicker. But dammit, he thought, it all happened so fast.

Later, when Mr. Harris left the store with his purchases, he said to Tom, "Mr. Rhee tells me that you a hard worker." He cleared his throat. "That's good. You watch yourself, T-Thomas."

Tom thanked him, and Mr. Harris walked slowly down the street. Mr. Rhee hurried out of the store after him. "Mr. Harris! You leave change on counter!" He brought the change and they talked briefly. He walked back.

"That Mr. Harris. He come here when the store first open," he told Tom. They watched Mr. Harris' thin figure stop at the corner, checking for cars.

"He seems like a nice man."

"Sad man," Mr. Rhee replied, shaking his head. "His wife killed two years ago by *gang-peh*. He always buy apples here. He takes home and cut so he can eat, but he like apples."

"How did his wife die?"

Mr. Rhee said, "*Gang-peh,* they grab her purse, push her down, but she old and can't get back up." He pointed to his heart as he walked back into the store. "Heart 'tack."

Tom saw Mr. Harris turn a far corner. While sitting on the stool and watching the few customers come in and out—sometimes placing the fruit in the thin plastic bags and weighing it on the hanging scale—he reached over and took a green apple. Living and working here is crazy, he thought. He wondered if the constant unease that he thought he felt got any better, if you became used to it. Or maybe once you lived here for a while, you saw that it wasn't really that bad.

Δ

After Tom was paid for the week he hurried out of the store and felt suddenly a small relief within him, as if he could inhale deeply again without being trapped. He couldn't stop thinking about those kids, and what would have happened if he had tried to stop them. He wasn't a security guard, wasn't a cop. Why did they expect him to do all that? Hell. He checked his pocket for the cash again, and crossed the street. Didn't matter. He had his money.

A heavy thumping of muffled music approached him, and he turned. On the opposite side of Amber a black Corvette drove slowly down the street, the heavy bass rhythm of the stereo vibrating the car and echoing in the streets. In the dusk light, the smooth, slick contours of the car body reflected shades of blue and purple, and the front window went down slowly, the music growing more loud and tinny, cymbals and a woman's singing now adding to the bass. A black man with sunglasses turned to look at Tom. The man took off his sunglasses slowly and stared at him, his eyes narrowing. Tom, surprised by this, looked away and worried that he had been staring. The car drove on, the beat warping as the car sped up.

Tom relaxed. He had to be more careful. He walked more quickly down Amber, towards his apartment. People were going home from work, cars driving in from New York, and he saw people walking into a bar, The High Tavern. Tom peered through the window and saw a crowd at the bar, ordering drinks, some more people at the tables along the wall, and he considered for an instant going in there to join them, but then continued on. Too crowded. Too many people. What he needed was quiet.

After he bought a sandwich and a beer at the deli, he came home and turned on the TV to fill the room with the news. He laid out his dinner on the coffee table and sat on the floor. The light on the ceiling, though working, wasn't very bright and he had begun leaving it off. He ate to the light of the TV, and his sandwich glowed.

He thought about tomorrow, and remembered that June would be there again. He realized that the store was often quiet and boring without her, and he found himself looking forward to seeing her again. She hadn't shown up last Sunday, the day after their first meeting, and though he hadn't noticed it until he left the store, he realized now that he had missed her.

Δ

"The pills?" Tom said. "Actually, they made me sick. Really sick."

"What? You're kidding!" June said. She shook her head. "I didn't know they were—"

"It's all right. I got over it." Tom waved his hand, though he felt queasy just thinking about it now. June picked up an apple and polished it on her T-shirt. They were out in front, Tom sitting on the stool and watching the customers that came in. June leaned against the door and tilted her head.

"So your father's in New Jersey again?" he asked, wanting to change the subject.

She nodded. "I think he found a deli that can be converted."

"A lot is riding on this, isn't it," he said.

"More than they let on. I mean, the bank and the *keh* will put—"

"The what?"

"They're just other businessmen like my father who pool and loan each other money," she said. "But this store here," she motioned inside with her head, "will pay for the other store, and everything's so risky."

"Your parents work hard, though."

"You do too. They said so."

Tom turned to her, uncomfortable with this. They talked about him? "What else do they say?"

"Not much. They don't know much about you."

"There isn't much to know."

"What about your parents?"

Tom hesitated. She leaned forward. He told her about his mother dying when he was five, and his father's more recent death.

"So your father raised you."

Tom cleared his throat and sat up. "More or less. Though right after my mother died my father sent me to California for a year, then to Korea for another year—I don't remember any of that—and I stayed with relatives."

"You've been to Korea at least," she said. "I haven't."

Tom shook his head. "I remember nothing. Those years are a blank."

"But you remember your mother."

He nodded.

"Wait a sec. You lived in Korea with Korean relatives, but you can't speak the language?"

"Can't understand it either," he said.

"That must have been weird."

Tom recalled only fragments of that time: his grandmother with three front teeth missing, her wrinkled sunburnt face yelling at him for breaking something and him crying; Tom looking out a window and seeing an old green rusty taxicab; a big meal at the table with Tom sitting on Bibles which hurt his bottom. But now that June mentioned it, he wondered how he had communicated with them. Maybe back then he had understood Korean, but he had since forgotten how.

Mrs. Rhee called Tom, and he jumped off the stool.

"You're pretty hyper," June said to him as he walked inside. He didn't answer.

"You take register now, okay?" Mrs. Rhee said.

Tom agreed and went behind the counter. He heard Mrs. Rhee tell June something in Korean, and she said, "I've been studying all morning!"

Mrs. Rhee said something again in Korean. June shook her head slightly and walked into the back room, her hair swinging against her shirt.

He settled back into the plastic chair. No

customers right now. Those questions from June bothered him, but he knew she was curious and let it go.
She's young, he thought, and nosy. But he liked
having her around.

Tom heard Mrs. Rhee say hello to someone, and then Mr. Harris answered. They spoke for
some time, and then Mr. Harris came in and waved to
him, putting his hands back into his jacket pockets, a
tweed cap on his head. "T-Thomas," he said, smiling.

Tom asked how he was.

"Just fine." He walked down the aisle
and June came out and said hello. Mr. Harris asked
her how school was going and if she was going to an
Ivy League college. Their voices lowered as June
walked with him to the refrigerated aisle.

Then, a muffled dance beat, synthesized
music coming from a car. Tom glanced outside,
wondering if it was that same car from yesterday.
No, he saw the front end of a white car, a shiny white
sedan. The door opened, letting out a wave of music,
then it slammed closed, muffling the beat again. Two
expensively dressed Asian men walked in. Double
breasted black blazers with padded shoulders, baggy
pants, one wearing large dark sunglasses, and the
other man checked his watch as they passed the
counter, the gold and silver flashing in the fluorescent light. They walked quickly to the back, glancing
at Tom, heading for the cases of beer in the refriger-

ated displays.

Mrs. Rhee stood by the door, looking in.

Mr. Harris approached the counter with a half-quart of Lactose reduced milk, while June returned to the back room. Mr. Harris looked curiously towards the muffled beats, then turned to Tom. "Th-this is all, thanks," he said, placing the carton next to the register. "How you doing?"

"I'm okay," Tom said. He checked the mirrors. The two men were pointing to different cases.

There was a honk from outside, and the one with the dark glasses pointed to a case of Budweiser. The other one grabbed it.

As Tom rang up the milk, the two men brought the case to the register, waiting behind Mr. Harris.

"One fifty-five," Tom said to Mr. Harris.

He nodded and reached into his pockets for his wallet. "Mrs. Rhee t-tell me you live 'round here."

"That's right. On Eisenhower."

A honk from outside.

Mr. Harris handed Tom one dollar and said, "Hold on. M-Might have change."

The Asian man with the gold watch sighed in annoyance. Mr. Harris, either not hearing this or choosing to ignore it, checked his front pockets and reached in, struggling, digging deeper, his body stooping over.

"We're in a hurry," the one with the sunglasses said.

"You sho' are," Mr. Harris said, not missing a beat. "A s-second, though." His bony hands pulled out scraps of paper—little torn notes with writing on them—along with change. Meeting Tom's eyes, Mr. Harris grinned. "That be enough?"

The one with the gold watch whispered, "W-W-We're in a h-h-hurry" to the other. They laughed. Tom felt his face flush as he took Mr. Harris' change. Tom noticed June was at the door, watching. His hands were sweating.

"T-Thomas," Mr. Harris said. "You have the lottery tickets?" He leaned in. "Got to be gettin' my million."

"Jesus," the one with the watch said. "Will you hurry up?"

"Do you mean the Lotto or the scratch off?" Tom hoped he didn't mean the Lotto, otherwise he'd have to use the machine and take more time.

"The scratch-off."

"That's a dollar," he said, reaching down to tear off a card. He ripped the perforation carefully, and gave it to Mr. Harris, who turned the card over and examined it.

"Come on, man."

Another honk.

Mr. Harris pulled out his wallet and searched for another dollar.

"Come *on*, man."

"Take it easy," Tom said.

The one with the watch glared at him. "They're waiting for us out there."

Mr. Harris handed Tom another dollar. "Is that all?"

Nodding, Mr. Harris thanked him.

Tom put the carton of milk into a bag and handed it to him. Before Mr. Harris had moved away from the counter, the others banged their case of beer onto the counter. Mr. Harris shook his head and walked towards the door. June walked outside, following him.

"Will you come on?" the one with the watch said.

Tom began to ring up the beer. "$14.06," he said.

"Took you long enough."

Looking at them for a second, he said nothing. Assholes. They pulled the case off the counter and hurried out. As they passed through the doorway, the one with the watch spat on the floor. The other laughed. They left the store and while the front door was closing, climbed into the car, the wave of music entering the store. A slam, and the music deadened.

Then Mrs. Rhee walked in, saw the spit, and glanced back outside, watching the car drive away. She looked down for a second, then went to the back to get a mop. Tom watched her clean the doorway slowly, her thick forearms pulling and pushing the mop back and forth in a steady, figure-eight motion.

FIVE

Although Tom did not witness the robbery, did not, in fact, even learn about it until the next morning, he has gone over it many times while lying in that hospital bed and thinks he knows, after all this time, how it happened. He was actually on a date with June during the robbery; yes, a date, and later, when he pieced together some of the events based on Mr. Rhee and June's account, he understood enough to try to push it from his mind, though he couldn't. Now, with long nights and days with nothing to do but think and remember and reconstruct, he imagines that evening from Mrs. Rhee's perspective, and sees much more. He sees Mrs. Rhee tapping her foot as he, the impatient clerk, leaves early. She knows that he is supposed to wait until her husband returns from New Jersey, but instead he, Thomas, leaves at seven every night. Sometimes Mr. Rhee is late because of a last-minute problem, but that does not matter to Thomas, she thinks, annoyed.

He says he has to be somewhere and he cannot be late three or four days a week just because Mr. Rhee is delayed, so she lets him go. But she does not like it. What is a few minutes? She feels like he is getting paid more than he deserves. She shakes her head. She will never understand him.

She rings up one of the few customers in the store. Although the afternoon was very busy, the evening is slower, and Mrs. Rhee is comforted by the electronic rings of the register. Sitting down after the customers leave, she sighs. She is worrying about the expansion: Mr. Rhee found a location and is beginning to set up the store, but he had to apply for a bank loan in addition to getting money from the *keh*. This means their monthly payments are going to be high, and they will depend on this store to cover it, at least until the New Jersey store can start showing a profit. Mrs. Rhee is feeling a pressure she has not felt since the Fruit 'N Food first opened over four years ago.

Δ

What was it like back then? Tom knows from talking with the Rhees that they risked all of their capital and borrowed heavily from relatives and a smaller *keh* since the banks hadn't thought they were a safe loan. They spoke of the extremely long and hard days when they had set up the grocery. Much of it had been through trial and error since they had not known anyone in the grocery business. Looking back, the Rhees could not believe how risky it had been. Eventually, their relatives had introduced them to some people who knew enough about the business to offer some good advice.

The first year had been the hardest. Stupid distributors, bad business decisions, and dealing with foreign customers had made that year terrible. One of the hardest things had been telling customers—mostly black women from the Carribean—that this store did not bargain for prices. They always wanted to haggle over everything, and it had taken many "All Prices Final" signs and continued refusals to lower prices. They lost many customers like that, but what did those people expect, the Rhees said. Most stores in the city do not haggle over prices, so why should they be any different? Maybe if they had better business at the time, if they did not have to count every penny, haggling might have been okay in some cases. But that first year every sale they made helped them get out of debt. They needed accurate records of sales, and changing the prices would have made that too hard.

In the second year, the Fruit 'N Food became part of the New York Grocery Association which let them get better deals on produce, and better advice. A Korean man who had been in the business for over ten years came and helped them for a few days. He showed them more efficient accounting procedures, and introduced the Rhees to distributors who worked with other Korean groceries in the tri-state area. After that, their store began doing better. Their profit margin doubled and their future looked secure. The expansion they were starting now was just the beginning for the Rhees. They wanted to make enough money for Jung-Me to go to an Ivy League college, and then maybe buy a house on Long Island. Maybe even retire early.

So, that evening while Mrs. Rhee waited for her husband, she thought about the expansion and checked the clock again, wondering where her husband could be. Now that he was definitely late, she felt less annoyed at Thomas for leaving—he would have waited too long if he had stayed. There were no customers at the moment, so she walked around the counter and went outside to cover the fruit. While pulling the clear plastic over the oranges, she noticed a slim man at the corner, leaning against the fire hydrant near the laundromat. His legs were crossed, and he slouched forward with his hands in his pockets. She stared for a second, not sure why this man was sitting there. She could not distinguish any features since he was in the shadows, but when she thought about the recent robbery two blocks up at the fast-food restaurant, she hurried inside and called Mr. Casey, who owned the laundromat.

"Hello? Mr. Casey This is Mrs. Rhee at

the Fruit 'N Food."

"Yeah? How's business?" He coughed away from the receiver.

"Good," she replied. "Are you okay?"

"What? Yeah, why?"

"There is man standing outside your store. You see him?"

"What? Hold on."

Mrs. Rhee heard the machines in the background. A whirring sound with an occasional burst of hissing. Probably a steam press. Her in-laws owned a laundromat, though she had visited it only once. After a minute, Mr. Casey came back on. "No. What you talking about?"

"No man there?"

"Uh-uh. There a problem?"

She apologized and hung up. When she peered out the door, she saw no one, so she switched on the outside floodlights which, although it wasted electricity, made the fruits easier to see from inside. The front sidewalk was now covered in light.

Where was her husband? Held up in traffic probably, though he was almost forty-five minutes late, and he should have called her by now. Mrs. Rhee walked back into the store, wondering if something had happened. When a young Latino couple walked in, she moved behind the counter, glad for the distraction. She glanced at the clock again.

Δ

While Mrs. Rhee worried about her husband, Tom was on his way to meet June. She had asked him right before his shift was over, and at the time he hadn't seen anything wrong with it, but now, while walking to the Meridian Café on the corner of Amber and Daly, he wasn't sure if he should go. For all he knew the Rhees thought he was some flunky charity case, and if they knew he was getting friendly with their daughter, they'd fire him.

But hell, he thought. He was hungry and he was going to eat. It didn't matter whom it was with. He approached the small café, passing a bakery which was closed right now, an empty display with yellowing paper lining the sides, and he saw some people in the Meridian window sipping coffee, others leaning back and reading a newspaper or a book. He walked in, inhaling the sweet coffee smells, and looked around. June was supposed to be here first. She left the store early, telling her mother that she was going to see her friend in Forest Hills, spending the night again. The café was dark, with small pale hanging lamps above each table. He saw a door leading to the patio.

Outside, each table had candles in red translucent bowls, little wicks burning in liquid wax, and Japanese rice paper lamps hanging from wires running high over the customers' heads, the soft lighting swaying back and forth with each breeze. He saw June in the corner, waving to him. She was wearing a light black sweater and jeans, and he felt slightly embarrassed now as people turned to see him...her dinner date. She didn't look as young as she had at the store; she wore her hair tied back, which, although it made her face look fuller, her cheeks fatter, made her look a few years older. She wore silver dangling earrings. He sat down across from her and glanced at the menu.

"I thought you forgot."

"No. Your mother wanted me to help with something. Your father still hasn't come back yet."

"Sometimes he's late," she said. She looked up. "Here's the waitress."

They ordered their dinners—croissant sandwiches and Tom had coffee—and fell silent. After a lengthy pause, Tom said, "What are your parents like, outside of work?"

"Outside of work? Nothing. Their whole lives are work work work."

"That's crazy."

"They're crazy, all right. I'm just glad they don't work me to death."

Tom didn't say anything.

"Even though it's like, they're doing all this for me, they say."

72

"For you."

"They want me to go to college and all that."

"Nothing wrong with that," he said.

"No, but they're putting a lot of pressure."

Their dinners came and they began eating, and their conversation continued about her parents. June mentioned that her father had gone to college in Korea; he had studied electrical engineering, but couldn't get a job here, so went into the grocery business. Her mother was going to be a nurse in Korea, but quit school to marry her father. Tom couldn't say much about his parents. Both his mother and father had studied in the States, and his father kept switching jobs for as long as Tom could remember.

"Do you miss them?" June asked.

"Not really," Tom said. "Sometimes I think about them, but that's about it."

"What was she like, your mother?"

Tom bit into his sandwich and thought about this while he ate. "I don't remember much, but she used to take me places. She liked to go out."

"But you don't like doing that, going out and all."

"Why do you say that?"

"Am I wrong?"

He shook his head. "You're right."

"Why?"

"I did in college, but got tired of it. Too many people make me uncomfortable."

June smiled and said, "Well, we can change that. You might actually have a good time."

He glanced at her, not sure if she was making fun of him, but she just grinned and continued to eat.

After they finished their sandwiches June asked, "Do you mind if I smoke?"

"You smoke?"

She nodded and pulled out a pack of Camel Lights. "That's why I got this outside table," she said.

Tom didn't comment. He watched her hold the cigarette in her index and middle fingers, in a "v", while she used her silver lighter. She inhaled and then puffed out a long stream of smoke. Somehow, she didn't look natural with a cigarette. "Do your parents know you smoke?" he asked.

She shrugged.

Just a kid, Tom couldn't help thinking. He ordered more coffee and noticed that the café was beginning to fill up.

"We can leave soon, if you want," June said. "I know this great bar near the Government Center. We can get a few drinks there."

He looked up. "But aren't you under—"

"Oh, I have i.d. and all that, and they really don't care."

Drinks. Tom wasn't sure about this.

"So why'd you leave Boston?" she asked.

Tom looked up. "A couple of reasons: my lease ran out and the restaurant was laying people off. I wanted something different."

"So you came back here, where you grew up."

He nodded.

"Well, you definitely got something different, working for my parents."

Tom smiled. "I like them, though your mother can be...." He worried about offending June. "...racist? Sometimes."

She shrugged again. "I don't know what your parents were like, but a lot of older Koreans are like that. They just don't know any better."

"But your mother," he said slowly. "She should know better, shouldn't she?"

June said, "You don't understand. If you come here thinking all blacks are in gangs, then your store is robbed by blacks, and and everyone's store is robbed by blacks, what're you going to think?"

"Yes," Tom said, "but—"

"I think my mom's racist, but I can understand it." She tapped some ashes onto the ground.

"You know, my parents are really glad you're working there."

"They are?"

"Especially now. You do twice what I did, and with my dad gone a lot, you're needed badly there."

"Really?" Tom had trouble believing this, but it made him feel good.

She glanced at the bill on the table. "Let's go."

Tom hesitated as June stood up and grabbed her purse.

"Just a drink, Tom," she said, waiting for him. "What else are you going to do tonight?"

He thought about that, and stood up.

Δ

With the store now empty, and with her husband still missing, Mrs. Rhee began checking the register receipts to pass the time. It was eight o'clock and the store would be closing soon, and she wondered if she should begin cleaning up, or if she should wait. A brief wave of anxiety passed through her as she pictured an accident on the highway, especially since she knew their car was old, and anything could happen to it, or maybe there was an accident at the other store. She dismissed this. He had been late before. He usually called, but today he might be stuck in traffic, unable to get to a phone.

The carbon copy roll of the daily receipts was inside the register, and Mrs. Rhee opened the small panel to check it. By turning the key in the register to "Total" she could make the machine print out the total purchases for that day. When she did this, the door bell let her know she had a customer. Looking up and seeing a black man in a dirty brown jacket with the collar up, and jeans that were ripped along both knees, Mrs. Rhee closed the register lid and stood up straighter. The skinny man was looking around the store, and walked slowly down the first aisle, his sneakers not making a sound. Mrs. Rhee was not sure, but this could have been the man she had seen on the corner. The way his shoulders drooped forward, a slight hunch, and the way his knees seemed to point inwards was familiar, but only vaguely so. It had been dark on the street.

The man walked across the refrigerated aisle, his steps slow and deliberate, looking at the drinks. He studied a bottle of soda for a while, tilting his head one way, then another. He began walking up aisle two, heading for the counter. Mrs. Rhee moved closer to the register, her foot inches away from the small red button next to the base of the counter.

Since she had been held up before, she trusted her instincts and she did not like this man. He looked nervous, not looking at her but instead staring at a vegetable can he kept turning in his hands. At the sound of the dehumidifier in the back room— a small automatic click and a low hum—the man whirled around. When he realized it was nothing, he glanced at Mrs. Rhee and then looked back down at the can.

Something was not right. Something about this man. Did he really want to buy something? Why was he waiting?

He put the can back onto a wrong shelf and began walking quickly towards her. Her heart began racing and she looked at the clock, at the door, and then at the man. She was beginning to panic. Mrs. Rhee saw his hand reach into his jacket and she immediately stamped on the alarm button again and again and again.

Δ

"All I remember is everything being white," he told her. He was trying to explain his nightmares.

"But what else? What was white?"

"Everything was. Everywhere I looked, it was really white. I don't know, maybe I was in Heaven."

June laughed through her nose. "A nightmare in Heaven? That's perfect."

They were approaching the Government Center, one of the taller buildings in Kasdan, built a few years before Tom had left. He remembered the construction here, the iron girders almost thirty stories high with huge cranes and the constant rumbling of jackhammers. This building held the local government offices, and he walked closer to it, he looked up and traced the building with the blank windows curving over him into the dark sky. A few windows were lit.

"Here it is," she said.

Tom followed her gaze and saw the bar, not really a bar since there was no sign over the place—it looked like it had been a regular store at one time, with a front display window and a glass door to the right. The glass was tinted but he saw the videos and some colored lights inside. He could hear the loud music, and he suddenly felt old, too old for this. When he was in college he had gone to bars like these, but had hated it then—music too loud, no one to talk to—and he couldn't see how anything had changed.

"I don't know about this," he said.

"Look, just a few drinks. I know some people here."

He followed her, reluctantly, and entered the nameless bar. Struck with the loud synthesized music and with the strong odors of sweat and alcohol, Tom stood at the doorway and watched June disappear into a crowd of people, customers here packed shoulder to shoulder. Almost everyone here was Asian and he thought this was strange. He worked his way to the bar and ordered whiskey—he needed something strong—and leaned against the sticky wooden bar and watched the video screens of people dancing and felt the thumping music in the floor, through his body, and he drank his whiskey quickly, his throat burning, and ordered another. June found him and pulled him into the crowd, introducing him to some of her friends, her young friends, and Tom thought, What the hell am I doing here? He could barely hear anyone over the music or see anyone in these lights so he didn't bother talking, but instead just drank and looked around him to the sea of black hair in the flashing lights and he began to feel lightheaded. As the night progressed he just drank more and the bar began filling up with dozens and dozens of people, the Saturday night party in full swing, the noise rising as people shouted to be heard. Larger groups of people formed; laughter, the center of attention shouting a story, smoking cigarettes, people dancing though there was no room and couples in the corners pushed up against each other, talking, drinking, kissing, and soon Tom was drunk and moving with June from group to group, listening in, though Tom just nodded his head and most people left him alone and everything became blurred as he and June danced closely, touching each other, and he thought that this didn't seem so bad.

Δ

The black man with grey teeth screamed at her to give him the money, his gun waving back and forth in front of her face. Mrs. Rhee was thinking how to stall him until the police arrived.

"*Mo? Hanguk mal.* No speak English," she said, reverting back to an instinctive strategy when she needed time to think.

"Fucking bitch! The fucking money!" The man swept the counter with his gun, knocking the candy jar and the key-ring display onto the floor, the glass crashing and the key-rings jingling across the linoleum. He glanced at the door and pointed the gun in front of Mrs. Rhee's face. The sound of the glass had shaken her, and now, watching the gun move back and forth, she realized she could be killed, and she thought of Jung-Me and her husband and she suddenly lost her sense of direction, and everything around her became blurry, and the man slapped her in the face, and she cried out and grabbed the counter as the man screamed again, "Open the register and get the money!"

Mrs. Rhee held her cheek in her shaking hands and felt for the register, her eyes stinging. She pressed the no-sale key, but it did not ring up. Instead, the electronic error beeped and she pressed it again and again, and she became desperate not knowing why this was not working now, when she needed it to, and she continued pressing it, the rapid beeping confusing her more. The man reached over the counter, grabbed her shirt, touching her breast and she pulled away in disgust. The man pulled her towards him and fiercely pushed the gun into her neck, choking her, and he said, "You think I'm stupid?" She smelled the oil and something burnt from the gun and the sweat running down his temple and she did not want to look him in the eye, so she looked at the stubble on his chin, white shaving scratches, dark acne marks, hard thrusts of day-old beard growing in.

He jumped over the counter, pushing Mrs. Rhee against the wall and she felt a sharp pain in her leg as she stumbled back over the chair and banged her head into the wall, an explosion of lights as she cried and fell into the seat, clutching the wall for support.

The man turned the key in the register, away from "Total" to "Sale" and the register beeped again, this time signalling it was okay. Mrs. Rhee had forgotten about the switch and she watched the man ring open the register and take all the bills, even the one-dollar bills, from the tray, stuffing them into his pockets, and then he lifted the tray up and grabbed the larger bills she had put underneath, the fifties, sometimes the hundreds, and she did not know how this man knew this. All the money from today went into his hand and Mrs. Rhee became furious at this *gumdngee* who was taking her money which the store needed, and she lunged for the cash in his hand saying in Korean that this was theirs, not his. The man stopped her with one fist to her chest which shocked the breath out of her, and he called her a chink bitch. With a sweeping, easy movement he brought the gun down on her cheek with a crack and everything blurred, this time forcing her to the ground, pain everywhere, and the store falling away around her.

She heard the man jump over the counter, his feet crunching on glass, and he ran away, the bell ringing as he left. She tried to lift her head up from the dirty, cold floor, but she felt sick and everything was spinning. The pain in her face burned. Opening her eyes and seeing a small puddle of blood on the floor—was that hers?—she tasted a salty wetness in her mouth; she hoped no customer came in and saw her like this. Where was her husband? It was so late.

SIX

Tom arrived at the store the next morning hung over, exhausted, and worried about last night. He had slept with June and now he wasn't sure what to do. As soon as he walked inside the grocery, Mr. Rhee approached him and said quietly, "From now on you must stay here until I come."

Tom tensed. Did Mr. Rhee know? There was a long, confusing pause while Tom tried to understand. "Okay," he said slowly.

"There was robbery here," Mr. Rhee said

"What?"

Mr. Rhee repeated it and shook his head. "After you leave and before I come, another robbery."

"Here?" Tom finally said.

"Black man had gun. Mrs. Rhee press alarm. The man hit her and take all money. She hurt on face and police come soon."

"Where is she now? Is she okay?"

"She stay home today to rest. Hurt just on face," he said, pointing to his cheek. "Today, you take care of store."

"By myself?"

"I have to check on Mrs. Rhee, then go to New Jersey—people waiting for me. Mrs. Rhee can't come. Jung-Me going home."

"You spoke to June?"

"Yes. She go home."

Tom waited, but there was nothing else. He studied Mr. Rhee and saw only worry and what seemed to be an anxiousness to leave. His body was poised towards the door, and Tom realized that Mr. Rhee had had to wait for Tom to arrive.

"I come soon," Mr. Rhee said.

"When?" Tom asked, alarmed at the responsibility. He had just started here. They'd leave him alone already?

"Afternoon?"

Tom hesitated, then said, "I guess so.... I better get to work then."

"Good," Mr. Rhee said, putting on his coat. "You take care of here."

"How long will Mrs. Rhee be gone?"

"Two day." Mr. Rhee stared at Tom for a second, then nodded. "You get paid more, okay?"

"Yes."

"Thank you, Thomas." He hurried out.

As Tom watched the door close in Mr. Rhee's wake, he rubbed his eyes and temples, his headache throbbing, and tried to organize his thoughts. So many things to do. Fruit stand outside, distributors might be coming in, cleaning. He went outside and began stacking apples in the wooden stand, finding the repetition soothing, rhythmic, with the one-two placement, rows upon rows, shiny reds, dull greens, bruises turned away—the apples had that sweet smell he liked, and he began to feel better.

Everything was so hazy last night because he had gotten drunk, but he remembered walking home with her, taking her to his apartment, then both of them in their drunkenness falling onto his mattress.

He tried to push this from his mind. He concentrated on the oranges where the bright colors reflected the rising sun and made his headache worse. Last night was unreal to him. He had woken up alone this morning and hadn't been completely certain it had happened. And now this, a robbery?

He hurried inside and looked around the store. Nothing seemed different. He went to the register and opened it. There was money inside, but that was for change. Mr. Rhee must have cleaned up before Tom had arrived. Had Mrs. Rhee been scared? Tom didn't know what he would have done if it had been him.

He saw some small pieces of glass on the floor and he noticed that the candy jars were missing, and the small display of plastic change holders had been hastily put back together. These must have been knocked over.

The gun? Why hadn't Mrs. Rhee used the gun? He checked under the counter. Yes, it was still here. Maybe it had happened too fast. Tom touched his cheek and imagined being hit with a gun. No, not him. He'd never let this happen. He'd shoot before anyone would hit him.

He continued to set up, and about half an hour later the phone in the back room rang. When he answered it, he recognized June's voice immediately. His heart jumped.

"Tom? Is my father still there?"

He hesitated, unsure if she was going to pretend nothing happened. "No. He left."

"So he's leaving you alone today?"

"Yes," Tom said.

"So," June began, and paused. "How are you feeling?"

"Tired. How about you?"

"Hung over. But I had a great time last night," she said.

Tom didn't say anything. He felt an odd mix of attraction and embarrassment, and thought, I must be crazy. What did I do?

"Tom?"

"What? Sorry. It's just all this happening at once. I'm a little confused," he said. "How's your mother?"

"She's doing fine. Are you okay?"

"I guess so," he said.

"You sound funny."

"I should to get back to work."

"It'll be okay, Tom. Just take it easy."

He said he would, and hung up. Returning to the stand and finishing with the fruit, he liked her concern for him, but all this was getting confusing. He couldn't date her, could he?

He finished the fruit and went inside to sweep around the counter, getting the pieces of glass Mr. Rhee had missed. A few teenager girls with similar hairstyles—long, curly hair held together with a large plastic clip on top—walked into the store, moving towards the small make-up section in the back of the second aisle. Then, a couple walked in, talking to each other in low voices. Two black men followed shortly. There were too many people to watch, and he glanced at the mirrors. The teenage girls looked in his direction, then turned away. Why were they acting nervous?

While ringing up the couple, there was laughing outside. Was the fruit okay? He strained to see, but the laughter was fading. He finished the couple and followed them out the door to check the stand. The rows of fruit seemed untouched. He returned to the counter, sweating already as the day warmed, and rang up the two black men, who bought bags of potato chips and cheese puffs. As he was punching in the prices, the teenage girls walked out without buying anything. They didn't even look at Tom as they passed the counter. Did they steal anything? He wanted to stop and ask them to open their purses, their jackets, but he hadn't seen anything taken. What if one of them had stolen something expensive, like the make-up brushes? He tensed as he tried to figure out what to do, but then it was too late as they left the store.

He had to calm down. The store was empty now. He leaned against the counter and surveyed the store. Everything was okay. He rubbed his temples again, his headache getting worse, so he opened a packet of aspirin from the second aisle and took a few.

As the morning wore on, he kept thinking about last night. He couldn't believe he had done that. The Rhees' daughter. And he remembered thinking while he was in bed with her, naked, him on top of her kissing her, that Mrs. Rhee might have looked like this when she had been younger. Smooth skin, small layers of fat along the waist and stomach. Large breasts that leaned away from the chest. Tom and June had had sex in the light of his TV, the sound off, and strange shadows fell between their bodies. Neither of them had said a word once they had sat on the mattress together, both staring blankly, drunkenly at the TV screen, not even sure what was on, and then Tom had lain in her lap, not intending to but just wanting to lie down and her legs had been in the way, and then she had leaned over and kissed him, and suddenly they couldn't stop. They just continued kissing and rubbing against each other until they started pulling at their clothes and Tom leaned into her, rubbing himself against her, and she tightened her grip around him. He kept his eyes open while he was kissing her, and saw the blue flashes of the TV reflecting off the wall, and though he was there with her beginning to take off his clothes, he felt strangely detached from all that, feeling her hands reach down and touch him, lightly, stroking him, and then putting him in her mouth, the surprising warmth, the wetness, moving up and down, and then climbing on him.

Now, as another customer came in, Tom thought that he could have been having sex not too long after Mrs. Rhee was robbed. He found something frightening about the image of him and June with the image of Mrs. Rhee being held up. He tried to shake this off.

When he had woken up this morning

with cotton mouth and a dull throbbing headache he had needed a half hour to go slowly to the shower and rest underneath its hot steam, recollecting events, remembering that he had blown most of his pay for that week on drinks for himself as well as others. He seemed to have become more generous as he became more drunk. What a damn waste, he had thought in the shower, trying to wake up.

In the early afternoon, after Tom had dealt with the lunch crowd, Mr. Rhee called to check up on him.

"It's kind of busy," Tom said. "But I'm doing fine."

"Good, Thomas." There was a pause. "I been thinking. Maybe you shift hours? Come later and work later?"

"How much later?"

"At least until I come back from New Jersey? I don't want Mrs. Rhee in store alone."

"I guess so."

They spoke for a little more until a customer approached the register. Tom said goodbye and hung up, though as soon as he did this, he realized that he would be working after dark, well into the night, and most of the robberies occurred at night.

Δ

Tom hurried home, glad to be done for

the day. While working there he had constantly imagined the customers trying to shoplift. He had had to watch everyone carefully. When Mr. Rhee had finally returned, Tom had been so relieved that he agreed again to show up tomorrow later, and to stay into the night.

He entered his apartment, finding it strangely quiet, and sat on his mattress to nurse his headache, which was still as bad as this morning. He considered having something to eat, especially since he hadn't eaten all day, yet his stomach hadn't quite settled after last night, and maybe he ought to just drink more water. He turned on the TV and lay down, listening to the news about recent gang activity, especially the shootings involving neighborhood Asian gangs against other local gangs.

He stood up and walked to the window, opening it and listening to the evening traffic noises. He knew it was going to be another long night. He sat on the windowsill, looking down at some people standing at the corner, waiting for the traffic light. Red tail lights and white head lights reflected off chrome bumpers, sparks flashing in the street. A car honked in the distance. The light turned green, the Walk sign flashed on, and the group of people began moving along the crosswalk, the stragglers catching up, reaching the other curb. He began shivering, though it wasn't cold, and he held his arms and cradled his body, shaking in the window, wondering what was happening to him.

A knock at the door.

Tom first thought it was a knock on the other side of the hall, a knock for someone else, but the knock repeated. He asked tentatively, "Who is it?"

"June," the muffled voice answered.

He froze. A number of thoughts went through his head: Why was she here—did she want to see *him* —what if her parents—maybe he shouldn't let her in—

"Tom?"

He hurried and opened the door. "Sorry," he said. In the darkened hall light, she was disguised by the shadows, and it wasn't until she stepped inside that he saw her smooth, slightly flushed face, and she turned to him, watching him closely.

"Are you okay? You look terrible."

Tom said, "I'm not feeling so hot."

"I'm sorry. I can't stay long—my friend is waiting for me. God, you're shivering!" She leaned in closer and he smelled her perfume.

"No, I'll be all right. I probably really need to rest."

"Come on. Let me put you to bed. I forgot you haven't been sleeping much. We probably shouldn't have stayed out so late last night."

The mention of last night made Tom uncomfortable. She must have noticed this because she then said, "Don't worry, Tom. We were drunk."

He glanced at her, surprised by this.

"Come on. Lie down. Let me get you some water."

Tom moved to the mattress and lay his head on his pillow. He felt better and was thankful for June.

"You've been working too hard," June said from the kitchen, the faucet running. She brought him a glass of water and placed it on the floor next to him. "I'm sorry I have to run, but I just wanted to say hello and check on you. You don't have a phone, do you?" She looked around.

"Never had a chance to get one."

"I didn't think so." She stood. "Will you be okay?"

He nodded. "I appreciate this."

"I'm not really doing anything. Should I tell my parents that you won't be coming in tomorrow?"

Tom sat up. "They sort of need me, don't they?"

She said, "Probably."

"No, I'll be in. Later, though. I'm staying later."

"I have to run now."

Tom said goodbye and watched her leave. He felt the sudden emptiness of the room as the door closed.

Δ

When Tom came into the store the next morning he was surprised to see Mrs. Rhee. The left side of her face was swollen and discolored, the purples and oranges spreading out from under the small white bandage taped like an "H" over her cheekbone. She had let her hair out of her bun and for the first time Tom saw her stringy, coarse hair, peppered with grey, falling loosely to her neck. She looked younger, and he wasn't sure why she always kept her hair in a bun. She tried to give him a lopsided smile, but winced.

He asked her how she was.

"Good," she answered. "I'm tough."

He said she was.

She laughed. "You stay later with me, yes?"

"At least until Mr. Rhee comes in."

"Much better. Need more in store at night, then *gumdngee* scared."

Tom said nothing, but nodded.

"*Tasut* —five robberies! Too much."

"Yes," he said, blinking, trying to focus. "Too much." He went to get his apron. "Weren't you supposed to stay at home today?"

She waved her hand, dismissing that. "I have to be here."

Tom took her place behind the register, and the rest of the morning passed quickly. During the noon-time rush, Mrs. Rhee took care of the fruit stand, occasionally helping customers, but spending most of the time on the stool. Tom could see her from the counter, and wondered if it was a good idea for her to be working so soon. Didn't she need more recovery time?

He rolled his stiff neck, and tried to concentrate on the customers, though they were a blur. The electronic beeps and the front bell had a numbing effect; he tried to become a robot, like the register, checking the prices, ringing them up, taking the cash, giving the change, bagging the goods. He moved quickly to keep the line moving, and soon he didn't even have to pay attention to the items. The prices showed up on the register themselves, bypassing him. Last night he had had the nightmares again. But this time he remembered more than just that whiteness; he remembered some color, a light blue, that of the sky, of the sea. The blue tinted the white for an instant, but it was enough for him to feel a momentary respite in the dream. He never thought he dreamt in color. He didn't know what it meant.

After a half hour at the register, Tom heard Mr. Harris talking with Mrs. Rhee outside.

Mrs. Rhee was telling him about the robbery. Tom heard Mr. Harris say, "Awful" every so often and "Drug addicts." He soon came in and, upon seeing Tom, said, "Poor Mrs. Rhee." He shook his head. "Her face looks real b-bad."

Tom agreed.

"City's going to hell. Drugs everywhere." He began to walk away and said to Tom, "You be careful."

More customers lined up at the counter. Where were all these people coming from? He looked around the store, his mind wandering, and saw in the convex mirror a white kid, a teenager, fingering a bottle of Budweiser, his body elongated and distorted. The brown bottle was one of the large 32-ounce kinds that usually sold well.

Tom hesitated when he saw the kid with the bottle, but continued ringing up the customers. The teenager was wearing black pants and a suede jacket with the sleeves ripped off. He looked around, but did not see the mirror in the corner. His dark brown hair fell over his eyes, so Tom wasn't sure if the kid was looking up or at the lower shelf. The kid picked up the bottle and examined it slowly.

Please, no, Tom thought as he rang up the last person on line. He checked if Mrs. Rhee was out there. She was. There were four other customers, including Mr. Harris, still in the aisles. He wiped the counter, but kept his eyes on the mirror. The kid had put the bottle down and was looking at the top shelf, moving closer. No, no, please don't, Tom said to himself.

A customer. Tom rang her up, not paying attention to the item, trying to watch the store. The kid glanced up and down the aisle, then in one quick motion grabbed the bottle and slipped it into his jacket. He buttoned it.

Tom's heart beat quicker. He had seen the whole thing in the mirror. The kid must have done this before, because it had been very smooth, very fast, but Tom had still seen it. Damn. What should he do now? The customer took her bag and left. The kid began walking slowly down the aisle, casually checking other things on the shelves.

Should Tom yell at the kid? Call Mrs. Rhee? He had to do *something* though.

The kid began walking down another aisle.

Another customer approached the counter. A man with a blue headband. The kid began walking past the counter, towards the door. Do something, Tom thought. Now. Do something.

"Excuse me," Tom said.

The kid kept walking.

"Hey!"

He turned to Tom. "What."

"What do you have in your jacket?"

Mrs. Rhee opened the front door.

"Got nothing in my jacket." He shrugged.

"I saw you put the bottle in your jacket. Take it out."

"Got nothing in my jacket," he said. The man with the headband backed away.

"Mrs. Rhee," Tom said. "This kid is trying to walk out with a bottle of beer without paying."

"Fuck you. I ain't got nothing."

"Let me see what's in your jacket."

"Got nothing there!" He began walking.

Mrs. Rhee stood in the doorway, and said to Tom. "Push alarm. Call police." The other customers were watching. Mr. Harris turned to Tom, waiting. Mrs. Rhee stepped forward into the store.

"Go fuck yourself, gook lady." The kid stopped.

Tom pressed the alarm with his foot, making sure he felt the click of the button. He pressed it again a few more times. "The police will be here," Tom said.

The kid tensed, then looked at Mrs. Rhee. "Fuck out of my way." He moved forward.

Tom came out from behind the counter and moved towards the kid, who turned quickly. "Back off."

Mrs. Rhee raised her voice. "Give back

bottle! I see it in jacket!" She pointed to the bulge in his left side. "Police will come. Give it back!"

"Fucking shut up!" He looked to his left and grabbed the metal stand with the snack foods, pushing it over. There was a loud crash and the pastries spread across the floor.

Mrs. Rhee began yelling, "Look what you—"

The kid ran towards the door and Tom jumped forward grabbing the end of the kid's jacket, but the kid slipped away and pushed into Mrs. Rhee, who yelled louder and hit him in the neck. The kid knocked her to the side but she then grabbed his jacket and held tightly, so as she fell to the ground she pulled him with her.

Struggling away from her, trying to shake her off, he yanked free, but the bottle flew out and arced in the air, spinning top over bottom and the head hit the doorframe, an explosion of shattering glass, foaming beer splashing, more shattering glass as everything hit the floor. Mrs. Rhee yelled something in Korean. A customer screamed.

The kid then bolted out the door and Tom chased him, jumping over the glass. He saw the jacket flapping back and forth as the kid pumped his legs and increased the distance between them. Too fast. Tom stopped less than a block down, out of breath, heart beating wildly, watching the kid turn the corner. Tom bent over and held his stomach. Cramps. He walked to the store, his legs aching, and saw Mrs. Rhee brushing herself off, Mr. Harris and a few customers helping her.

He asked her if she was okay.

She nodded and said, "He get away?"

"Yes."

She sighed and stared at the beer spilling into the store. She sighed again and her face sagged, aged in the last ten minutes. She touched her bruise carefully, tenderly, then looked up at Tom. "You do good. He crazy boy."

He looked at the shattered bottle in the store entrance: the golden beer and the white foam seeped into the doormat, chunks of glass sticking up with smaller bits scattered around, the strong smell rising up to him. His eyes watered. He heard a siren in the distance. His heart wouldn't stop pounding and he was still shaking slightly, a tremor in his arms, in his legs.

SEVEN

The days passed at the store, and Tom seemed to feel worse. Now, while going over those events, Tom understands more, that the lack of sleep and the stress of the grocery, of June, were converging on him, pushing him. All he knew at that time, though, was that something was wrong. He remembers that one day when he lost control, when everything was so confused and blurred. It really began that afternoon while he sat outside the store watching the fruit, and he heard a slight buzzing in his ear, and his head pounded from a caffeine headache. He was drinking too much coffee since he had barely slept at all the night before, when he had simply watched TV the entire night, lying on his mattress, his head turned towards the glowing screen, vaguely following but not really watching reruns, sitcoms, late night talk shows, and an odd yoga show at five in the morning. He had been suspended in an agonizing state of exhaustion without relief, sleepiness without sleep, and after the sun had begun rising and shining into his room, he had blinked repeatedly, unbelieving, thinking, No, not already, it couldn't be. Ever since that shoplifting incident a few days ago, he had been sleeping less and less, until last night when he had had only a few minutes, it seemed, of rest.

His throat felt scratchy from breathing through his mouth all day, and it seemed, in the late afternoon sun which was too warm, too bright, forcing him into the shade, it seemed to him that if he didn't get some sleep soon he'd have to see a doctor, get some medication, or *something* or he wouldn't make it another week. Or maybe he had slept last night but had dreamed he'd been awake, and now he wasn't sure what was real or imagined, nothing was what it appeared anymore. No, he hadn't been asleep. Otherwise he wouldn't have been a zombie today, not fully aware of anyone or anything around him, moving and working from rote and paying attention only to the clock on the wall, watching the second hand move slowly over the numbers, the minute hand inching along every time he turned away, and the hour hand dragging at a tortuous pace, 11, 12, 1, 2, 3, 4, 5.... Only a couple more hours to go, he thought. He could do this. He could make it.

His vision was playing tricks in the low sun. Objects wavered under his gaze—telephone poles, street signs, parked cars—and he had to blink a few times, violently, for everything to keep still. He shook his head again, the pain in his temples sharpening his focus, and he took a few deep breaths.

Yesterday he had kept talking to June about that kid who had tried to steal the beer. She came over again and he was so glad to see her, so glad to have some company that he tried to make her stay longer even though she had to return home. Why did the kid want a bottle of beer, Tom kept asking her. Was he an alcoholic? For fun? To sell for some small change? June kept saying, I don't know Tom. You really need to get some rest. Let me get you some warm milk or something. Tom thought about the look on the kid's face when Tom had told him about the police, the startled look of fear and anger, as if surprised that these gooks had the nerve to call the police. That little shit, Tom said to June. But what if he had had a gun or knife? Take it easy Tom, was all June had replied.

Who was that? A man walking towards him. A customer? A big Latino man, tight T-shirt, a beard growing in. Why was he looking at Tom like that? What the hell was he staring at. Oh, he was looking at the fruit prices. He approached the store, walking past Tom. Seemed okay. Calm down. No reason to get anxious. Just take it easy. So jittery. Close your eyes and relax. Cars driving by, swishing, the sounds of tires on the road, sounding like waves—

Running. Tom sat up quickly and saw two kids running down the street, their sneakers slapping the sidewalk, a bright yellow tennis ball passing back and forth between them. The blond-headed one had a stickball bat. The one with a Mets baseball cap was laughing. They continued up the street while Tom watched them weave around pedestrians, race across the street. Tom was sweating, his breathing shallow. A painful heaviness in his chest.

The sky was beginning to darken, so he turned on the outside lights, though he really didn't have to yet. Mrs. Rhee came out and said they can switch places if he wanted to. He wanted to.

A commotion down the street. Yelling, arguing. The owner of the laundromat was throwing someone out of his store. The customer, a young man, cursed at him and said he was going to sue. The laundromat owner laughed and said something harsh. They separated, the owner still laughing. Tom watched the young man continue to curse as he walked across the street.

Maybe the whole city's uneasy, Tom thought as he walked inside. Maybe Mr. Harris had been right and everyone felt tense, unhappy, on edge, and maybe like that man on the corner of Amber and Banks had said a while ago on his soapbox, holding the New Testament in one hand and a bullhorn in the other, "Judgement is coming. The end is coming. We must repent."

Tom looked at the clock and saw that he still had two hours left, at least, so he poured himself a cup of coffee, and tried to relax since the store was relatively empty except for a customer looking at the hair and skin goods—a middle-aged man with a goatee and wire glasses putting a bottle of shampoo in his basket—and Tom added five spoonfuls of sugar because he was sick of the taste of coffee but he needed the caffeine otherwise he might not make it until eight. He better take it easy since rush hour was any minute now. The man walked to the counter so Tom put the coffee down and rang the man up who asked how he was, and Tom said he was fine but there was a slight waver in his voice which made the man cock his head but he didn't say anything, so Tom remained quiet. The man took his change and his bag and when Tom tried to get the receipt he found that the register had not printed it, or maybe it had but it was jammed, but the man nodded to Tom and left. He was balding in back. He didn't want a receipt?

Tom tried ringing up zero sales to get the receipt working but nothing came out except a choked whirring sound and he called Mrs. Rhee who saw him examining the register and she said, "It happen before. Mr. Rhee can fix. Just write out if they want receipt."

He replied that it was fine and she looked at him strangely but then returned outside, and Tom began writing out blank receipts on the white pad of paper to prepare for anyone who wanted one by printing carefully the store name on top, the date, the cost of item, and his signature on bottom. He became creative and used different colored pens, even mixing colors in the name of the store so that "Fruit" was one color and "Food" was another. His stomach churned with sour coffee.

Then a few customers came in and he rang them up making sure they got a receipt if they wanted one. He said he was sorry but the register wasn't working correctly, should he give them a hand-written receipt? Were they sure they did not want a receipt? Okay, that was fine, but if they decided they needed one they shouldn't hesitate to ask. Yes, he was fine, why did they ask?

While putting away the cash he wondered if he'd see June again this week, since summer school was taking up her time. June. He wasn't sure if he liked her or if he was just so lonely that he liked having her around, but one thing was certain: the Rhees couldn't know that their daughter was spending time with him, otherwise he could lose this job. What was he doing? She was too young, anyway, but every time he thought about her and that night they came back from the bar and she'd taken him in her mouth he became excited and though they hadn't done anything since then, he could feel the strange attraction whenever he saw her. This was crazy. Maybe he should just start stashing away money and try to get the hell out of here as soon as he could because something was happening even though he didn't know what but he didn't like how he was feeling—

More customers. Here came the rush. Six, no seven for now. No more please. No. Eight. Not yet. Too many people to watch, got to check each one carefully. Make sure that—Marlboro? A carton? Would that be hard or soft pack? Here you go. The register isn't working properly would you like a hand-written receipt? No? Okay, that's fine. Good evening will this be all? The register isn't working properly would you like a hand-written receipt? No? Have a nice night.

The customer left and Tom tallied the cash in his hands, dropping some change on the floor. Damn. He crouched down and tried picking it up, having trouble lifting the change off the floor since his nails weren't long enough and he kept pushing the coins away instead of grabbing hold of the edges, and he remembered having the same trouble at that bar with all the Asians there and he had been drunk and trying to pick up change from the bar but everything had been too slippery, or he had been too drunk, but it had been the same thing, and right now while stooping under the counter and collecting the fallen change he remembered that feeling he had had in the bar, that drunk, confused feeling with his head swimming and June had held his arm and had guided him all around the bar, to her many friends it seemed, and he had tried to act natural but had hated being there, Let me go, he had thought to her, Let me leave, but she hadn't until they had both been sick of it, and then they had stumbled back to his apartment where—

"*Aigoo!* I see you! I see you!" Mrs. Rhee yelled from the door and Tom dropped the change and his face flushed and a rush of fire burned his chest as he stood up and saw her, but she wasn't looking at him, and he tried to steady himself, his slamming heart. She was looking at a black couple at the snack food rack.

"I see you take food! I see you!"

The two customers who wore similar thin leather jackets and jeans looked at each other then at Mrs. Rhee, who hurried to them, and the man with a design cut into the side of his hair said something to the woman, then looked curiously at Mrs. Rhee.

Mrs. Rhee yelled, "Put back! Put back!" waving her finger and pointing to the woman while the other customers looked on, but the woman, shrugging her shoulders and shaking her head, said, "Hold up. We ain't took nothing."

"I see you take food!" She pointed to the cloth handbag under the woman's arms.

"What you talkin' lies for? What you lyin' for?" The woman was getting angry, her chin jutting forward, her hands on her hips.

The whole scene was blurry, so dream-like, that the voices didn't sound real and the faces distorted and enlarged and contracted as Tom tried to focus on them, and he watched Mrs. Rhee grab for the bag, lunging forward, hand like a claw, but the woman pulled it away and the man stepped between them, the woman screaming, "Don' you be touchin' my things, bitch!" and the man saying to Mrs. Rhee, "Hold up. Take it easy." But Mrs. Rhee did not seem to hear them—all she wanted was the bag—and she yelled, "You put in bag! I see you!" and pushed past the man and lunged again for the bag, but this time the woman pushed Mrs. Rhee away into the shelves, cans of soup crashing onto the floor and amidst the clatter Mrs. Rhee cried out in pain and she called out distinctly, clearly, without a trace of an accent, as if fear and pain forced her to be perfectly understood, as if this moment both she and Tom had known each other forever and one word connected their lives— she called out distinctly and clearly his name.

Tom was partially shaken out of this

dream, and he realized that she had been pushed to the ground and he didn't think, didn't plan, and he saw himself reaching for the gun, pulling it out quickly, clumsily, knocking over a box of coupons and the bags, and he heard Mrs. Rhee yell, "Thomas! Push alarm! Call police!" but he was already past the counter and running towards them because he could only think of a robbery and he did not want to be hurt and held up and beaten or shot so he had to stop anything and anyone who tried to rob them, and he waved the gun and heard someone yell, "He's got a gun!" and someone shouted and people jumped to the ground and he ran straight for the couple aiming the gun at them and the man looked confused, seeing the people drop around him until he saw Tom running to him and his eyes widened and he backed away but Tom moved forward and aimed the gun at the woman and yelled, Give it back give it back and don't ever touch her again do you hear me don't ever touch her again!

The gun was shaking in his hand and he couldn't seem to aim it straight but he held it with both hands now and the store was silent except for the black man holding both his hands towards Tom saying in a slow, quiet voice, "Don't do nothing stupid" and he made slow-down motions with his palms, stroking the air, telling Tom to calm down take it easy chill out, and the woman was not moving at all, a statue staring at the shaking gun, but the man had Tom's attention and Tom watched his hands and thought how they reminded him of waves at the ocean like when he had been at Jones Beach as a kid and the waves were calming, soothing, like this man's hands, and the sounds of the ocean and the voices and the lifeguard's shrill whistle and the man's voice soothed him, like the ocean and Tom began to breathe again, he guessed he had been holding his breath, and everything was coming back into focus and his own hands steadied and he realized where he was—he was not at the beach—and he took a deep breath and the man seemed to relax more and this made Tom feel better and he began to take his finger off the trigger slowly and he lowered the gun, carefully, slowly, and he left it at his side.

The man grabbed the woman and she said, "That crazy sucka could've wasted—" but the man hissed at her and whispered in her ear and pulled her along. She was still watching the gun at Tom's side. Mrs. Rhee was now watching him, not them. She did not stop them. Other customers hurried out.

"Maybe you go home now, okay?" Mrs. Rhee said. "Maybe you rest?"

Tom nodded, and put the gun into his pants. He walked out of the store and Mrs. Rhee said, "You give gun?" but he didn't really hear her and all he could think about was going to sleep, and he walked home in a daze.

For the first time since he had arrived here in Kasdan, Queens, Tom would go to his apartment, lie down on his mattress still in his clothes, close his eyes, and feel himself sinking away instantly, falling into a deep, quiet sleep.

EIGHT

"So you lose temper?" Mr. Rhee asked. "You lose temper when they push Mrs. Rhee?"

Tom nodded, certain that he was about to be fired.

"But you use gun. You point to customer. You scare other customers."

"I know," he said. "I lost control."

"Where is gun?"

"I left it at my place. I'll bring it back."

"Why you scare everyone?"

Tom shook his head. "I wasn't feeling well. I didn't want what happened to Mrs. Rhee to happen to me."

Mr. Rhee stared at him. "This not happen again."

"I know."

"If something like this happen again, you have to leave."

"Yes."

"No more scare customers," Mr. Rhee said. "Even if to help Mrs. Rhee." He picked up some folders and waved quickly to Mrs. Rhee.

Tom breathed easier once Mr. Rhee left, and he knew he had gotten off easily. Most of last night was unclear, but he realized he could have done something really stupid, like pull the trigger. And now that he thought about it, he wasn't quite sure where he had left the gun. He shook his head. What a stupid thing to do. He tried to push this from his mind while he stretched his back, holding the door for support. Despite the sleep he had had last night, his body still ached. He wasn't as tired, but his back and legs felt knotted with cramps.

Mrs. Rhee glanced at him from behind the counter. She and Tom hadn't spoken to each other yet, and he didn't know what to say, ashamed of his actions. What did she think of him now? *He* didn't know what to think of himself, losing it like that. What the hell had happened? Mrs. Rhee then called to Tom, telling him that she was tired and asked if he would take the register.

He told her he would. When they passed each other he said that her bruise looked better— some of the swelling had gone down. She nodded. "Feel better?" she asked.

He said he did. She brought a stool outside and propped open the door. When he settled in behind the counter he noticed that the receipts were printing out now. Mr. Rhee must have fixed it. At the side of the register were the prepared receipts Tom had made last night. The lines were dark and deeply imprinted in the paper. The handwriting was in block letters, as if a child had written all in capitals. He quickly crumpled these and threw them out. He cleaned the counter and rearranged the coupons and lottery tickets.

About two hours later, while he was with a customer, he heard Mrs. Rhee calling out to someone. "What you do there?" she said. But he didn't hear an answer. She said it again and the customer glanced towards the door. "Hey. You!" she called out. "What you do?" Tom couldn't see anything, so he finished with the customer and hurried to the door, his heart beating quickly.

"What's wrong?" he asked, and he immediately saw why she was yelling. Along the edge of the large sidewalk and in the street directly in front of the store, five people—four men, one woman, all black—were putting together picket signs and unfolding a small banner. Tom read "Boycott" on the banner. They were stapling poster boards onto long pieces of wood, inserting a broomstick into a banner where the top had been folded over and stapled, and they did this without looking up. Mrs. Rhee told them to do this somewhere else, but they ignored her. One person jogged to the small blue hatchback across the street, opening the back, and pulled out another sign post.

Mrs. Rhee said something under her breath and squinted, concentrating on one of them. Tom asked her what was the matter and she pointed to the man next to the woman. "That is man from yesterday."

He was wearing a windbreaker jacket and sunglasses, but Tom recognized the markings on the side of his afro—jagged lines, parallel lightning bolts. The woman finished pushing the broom handle through the banner and she glanced up, looking directly at Tom. Their eyes locked for a second and he looked away.

Mrs. Rhee said, "Tell them to go away."

"Me?"

"Yes. Tell them to go somewhere else."

"I think they want to picket the store."

"Pick? What is pick?"

"Picket. Protest. Maybe they want to boy-cott."

"What!" she said. "No. Go talk." She pointed to them. "Tell them we want to talk."

"Mrs. Rhee," he began, dreading this.

"Go now."

Tom hesitated, and glanced over to them. They seemed to be waiting for someone. He walked over to them slowly. The woman saw him and whispered to the man.

"Excuse me," Tom said. He was about five feet away from them. One person looked up at him for a second, then went back to his stapling. Tom said it again.

They ignored him.

"Mrs. Rhee, who owns this store with her husband, wants to talk about this. If there's anything—"

"Watch out," the woman said to the others. They turned to her. "This is the guy with the gun." She snickered.

"If you've got a problem, maybe we can talk about this."

"Where be Levar?" one of the men said to another. "Always fucking late."

"*We* ain't got the problem," the woman said, looking up at the sky. "Uh-uh. *We* be mindin' our business when Bam!" She punched her open palm, rolling her shoulders, her silver loop earrings swinging quickly up then down. "There be a fuckin' gun in my face." She looked squarely at Tom. "*We* ain't got no problem."

"Last night was a mistake," he said. "I thought Mrs. Rhee was going to get—"

"We want respect!" a man who hadn't spoken before said. He took off his sunglasses. "We are sick of this racism, 'cause that's what it is—pure and simple—racism!"

"You tell it, Robbie," another man said.

"You come in here," the man called Robbie said to Tom in a loud voice. He was wearing a white shirt with a striped blue tie. "You come in here and *suck* the money from the neighborhood and take it to your Long Is-land house and treat us African brothers and sisters like we nothing. Like we nothing."

"What're you talking about? I—I don't live—"

"But we are *something*. We are everything. We are your money, your customers, your nice car, your college education. So we want to be treated right. We want the respect we deserve."

"That's right," the woman said.

"We want the respect *everyone* deserves. *We want respect!*" He raised his sign and pumped it. "We want respect!" He held it up high. "We want respect!"

They all joined in, lifting the signs. "We want respect!"

Tom turned to Mrs. Rhee, but she had gone inside. He began to back away, reading the signs. Buy Black. Black Power. This Store Discriminates. BOYCOTT THIS STORE. Fair Treatment for ALL.

He walked back into the store, where Mrs. Rhee was ringing someone up. She turned to him. "What they do now?"

"They're protesting. They didn't want to talk."

The customer, while taking his purchases, cocked his head to the "We want respect" chant. When he left, Mrs. Rhee frowned. "I call police before. They send someone."

When Tom looked outside, the five were pumping the signs and banner in unison, still chanting, but with only five people, it didn't look threatening.

Curious onlookers slowed to read the signs, but moved on. Tom couldn't help thinking about last night, and how his stupidity had caused this. But what could he do about it now?

Mrs. Rhee asked him to take the register. She sat outside on the stool and watched the protestors. They had changed their chant. "Boycott Racism" was their new one.

A police car drove up about fifteen minutes later, and pulled over to the curb across the street. Two uniformed policemen climbed out, one black, one white, and walked over to Mrs. Rhee. Tom watched through the window. He hoped she wouldn't say anything about last night—could he be charged with something? The protestors grew louder, and waved their signs vigorously. The black policeman was older, with heavy wrinkled bags under his eyes.

They spoke with Mrs. Rhee who pointed to the picketers and then pointed to the store. The younger policeman shook his head and said something. He motioned to them and to the store and made a width motion with his two open hands, explaining something to her. She shook her head and said something more. He nodded to his partner, who went to speak with the protestors. Tom walked out. The white policeman glanced at him and continued.

"So as long as they keep that distance, and don't damage anything or stop customers, they're allowed to do this."

"They damage business if they stay," Mrs. Rhee said.

The policeman sighed and looked at Tom. "Hey, you speak English?"

Tom blinked. "Of course I do," he said.

"She don't seem to understand that what they're doing is legal."

The chanting stopped while the other policeman spoke with the protestors.

Mrs. Rhee said, "I understand. But they hurt business. Scare customer."

"But I can't do anything unless they break the law. I can warn them—that's what my partner's doing now."

They looked at his partner. The one called Robbie was speaking, gesturing emphatically, his voice rhythmically punctuated with highs and lows. The policeman nodded and shrugged. He walked back.

Rolling his eyes to his partner, he said, "They plan a peaceful demonstration this morning. They'll be leaving at noon."

Mrs. Rhee nodded her head.

"But," the policeman went on, "they'll be back tomorrow, probably with more people."

"*Aigoo*," Mrs. Rhee said. "More!"

The younger policeman said, "Well, we can send someone over tomorrow to check, but there's not much we can do." He paused. "Unless they block traffic or something."

"Or get violent," the other one added.

Mrs. Rhee thanked them and they left. The protestors began chanting again, this time just "Boycott." Tom and Mrs. Rhee tried to ignore them as they continued working—he at the register, Mrs. Rhee in the back room occasionally checking the fruit outside and sighing when she saw the boycotters. After a while, though, the chants became the background noise, and, strangely, they turned soothing, almost hypnotic with the rhythms of the voices. It was only when they changed their chant or one of them gave a speech to a passer-by that Tom realized what was really happening.

Like the policeman had said, the protestors began packing by noon. Mrs. Rhee and Tom watched with relief. They stood at the doorway as the signs were stacked and the banner rolled up. A few of them talked for a minute, then they separated, two leaving by car, three by foot. It seemed as if the one they had been waiting for never showed up. Perhaps this was a good sign. Mrs. Rhee pointed to some of the pieces of paper, the tape, and wrappers on the ground where the protestors had been and she told Tom that she would sweep this up. Tom thought he heard something accusatory in her voice, and he felt a guilty pang. He nodded and tried to immerse himself in the work.

By evening when Mr. Rhee returned, Tom was taking inventory. Mrs. Rhee was outside and talked with her husband for a long time. Tom finished recording the number of canned vegetables sold this week, and went back to the register and checked the daily totals. It had been a slow day. When Mr. Rhee came in, he paused, and asked Tom about this morning.

Deep creases formed on his forehead as he listened to Tom. He rubbed his eyes, his neck, and sighed. Shaking his head when Tom finished, he said, "This is bad."

Tom was quiet.

"They come back again?"

"That's what the policeman said."

"Mrs. Rhee say more will come," he said. "We have to make sure this do not get too big."

He asked how.

Mr. Rhee shook his head. "Not sure. You can go now," he said.

Tom thought about apologizing, or saying something to make Mr. Rhee feel better, but he didn't know what to say. He left quickly.

Δ

Tom heard June's knock at his door, and he told her it was open. She entered, slightly out of breath, and said, "I was just at the store. What's been happening?"

"Hi," he said, sitting back down on his mattress. "You heard about last night."

"And today. There were protestors?"

He nodded. "Not that many, but they're coming back tomorrow."

"So what happened?"

He told her briefly about being almost crazy without sleep and losing control when her mother yelled for help. While he was talking June sat down next to him, bouncing him up and down on the mattress.

"That's terrible," she said when he finished. "How are you feeling now?"

"Okay. I'm worried, though."

"About the protestors?"

"What do your parents think?"

"They don't know yet. It's still too early, but my mom is freaking. She keeps telling my dad to do something, but he doesn't know what to do either."

"What a mess." Tom rubbed his temples. Was all this really happening? "What a goddamn mess."

"They've had problems before," she said.

"Like what?"

"Once, my mom saw a black girl trying to steal something—I don't know what—and the girl hit my mom, who hit back. Then the girl sued." June turned to him. "The girl's lawyer tried to settle, but dropped it once he found out that we had witnesses. But we got a bunch of letters and threats."

Tom didn't say anything. So maybe all this wasn't his fault. Maybe he was only a small part of it. Then he suddenly thought of something. "Do your parents know you're here? Don't they wonder?"

She shook her head. "I sleep over at my friend's a lot, especially if I have school. It's closer."

Tom then wasn't sure if she planned to sleep over. He stared at her finger as she scratched a small hole in her cut-off jeans, running her nail along the frayed edges of the hole, circling it. There was an awkward silence, and he didn't want to think about the store anymore, about the Rhees, and he wanted right now only to stay here with June and though in the back of his mind he knew he was making a mistake, he moved closer to her and put his hand on hers. There was a moment when he was afraid she would pull away, but she didn't, and she leaned towards him, her shoulder touching his. He turned to her and kissed her. She kissed him back, and they fell slowly back onto the mattress, still holding each other, June laughing when they bounced. He moved on top of her and held her throat, the smooth ridges of her larynx beneath the web in between his thumb and forefinger, and leaned in. They faced each other, and she pulled him closer as they kissed again, their lips first dry but then wet and then pushing against their teeth, moving up and down, side to side. He became excited, thinking, This is crazy, but not being able to stop and his hands stroked her neck, the back of her head slowly, faint traces of perspiration against his fingers, and his breathing quickened as he rubbed against her jeans. He unzipped her quickly, then moved up and pressed his cheek against hers, and he felt her smile.

"Wait," she said quietly. A tiny breath in his ear.

He asked her what was wrong.

She told him she couldn't, not for a few days.

Confused at first, he then felt her pad, crinkling underneath her pants, and asked if it mattered.

"Messy," she said.

He continued kissing her. "I don't care," he said, "if you don't." He felt her shake her head and hurry to take off her clothes, first her shirt and bra, then the cut-offs, and Tom quickly stripped and ran his fingers over her body, letting his fingernails follow her contours, barely touching her soft skin, and she shivered as he drew circles over her stomach and along her ribs, zig-zagging over her breasts and back down her sides. Her skin was warm, and he ran the edges of his fingernails up her side, under her arms, as she arched her back and squirmed. He drew more circles, then wrote messages on her back, knowing she wouldn't be able to decipher them but it didn't matter, and he couldn't wait any longer and moved in between her legs, but she stopped him and closed her eyes, her arms reaching down in a "v", licking her fingers then going back down, touching herself, and after a minute she pulled Tom down and when they lay against each other, he felt her tighten her grip around his waist as he rested up against her, rubbing up and down to make sure it was okay, and then he eased himself inside her, holding her tightly as he felt her softness and heat wrap him and he almost collapsed on her thinking how good she felt, staring at the dull white wall for a second before he buried his face in the pillow and he felt her breath in his ear.

After he came Tom stayed inside her, resting quietly, listening to her breathe, and feeling the dampness on her face and neck. He apologized for not waiting, but she interrupted him before he finished and said it was okay. He felt stupid for rushing, but he wasn't drunk this time and couldn't stop himself. An odd smell of perfume and sweat filled him. He blew a jet of air onto her temple and her hair, cooling her. She smiled with her eyes closed. Tom liked the feeling of being inside, the slippery warmth, the aching relief, and he didn't want to leave. He was still sweating from the heat of her body, and every part of him that was touching her became even hotter.

He heard her steady breathing and asked her quietly if she was asleep.

She shook her head, her eyes still closed. She moved an arm away and Tom felt cold. He held her tighter.

"Tom?" she whispered. "Maybe you better pull out."

He asked her why.

"I'm bleeding," she said.

He had forgotten about that, and began to leave her, his body shivering. He touched her chest and felt the same slickness he sometimes had after he woke up from a nightmare.

When he looked down at himself, he jumped.

"What's wrong?" she asked, reaching for her panties.

Tom rose and showed her his mid-section streaked with her blood. His groin and lower abdomen were smeared with circular patterns of red, and his still hard sex was covered with a mix of blood and semen, dripping onto his leg. June hesitated, squinting at him, and apologized. She quickly put on her panties, pushing her pad against her, and Tom saw the blood on her upper thighs as well. She cursed when she saw the sheets.

He shook his head and said it didn't matter. With the blood dripping down him, he stared at himself curiously. He looked like he had been in an accident, the blood his, not hers. She grabbed a tissue and handed it to him. As he cleaned the blood off him, he felt a strange sadness overcome him. He watched her wipe her leg in parallel lines, a methodical cleansing, and he looked down and saw a drop of blood on his foot. June pulled the bedsheet off the mattress, and rolled it into a ball, the large bloodstain still visible in the crumpled mass.

NINE

Because he wanted to see the protestors, Mr. Rhee was staying at the store for the morning. Tom also thought he might have a plan to deal with this. Mr. Rhee spent most of the morning on the telephone, and except for a few words of direction, everyone was quiet, serious, and Tom found the tension painful—he tried to block it out by working harder. And he thought about June. He had left her sleeping in his apartment this morning, even though he knew she had to go to school; he hadn't wanted to wake her because she had been so still, barely even breathing, and he couldn't disturb that. He was glad she stayed, though. He liked having her there.

When Tom heard talking outside, he and Mr. Rhee checked and saw the protestors beginning to set up on the sidewalk and street again. Tom recognized the couple and the one called Robbie, but he wasn't sure if he saw the others from yesterday. Now there were nine. Mr. Rhee glanced at his wife, and she nodded. Mr. Rhee walked out to them, his bulky body moving slowly.

One of the protestors nudged Robbie. He looked up from the poster he was writing. Mr. Rhee asked them if they wanted to talk. Robbie said there was nothing to talk about. Mr. Rhee's voice lowered, and Tom couldn't hear what he said.

"It is *too* late for that. Talk is useless. It's time to act," Robbie answered.

"But you give no chance to talk. Just want to fight," Mr. Rhee said.

"Money is the only way you people talk. So we're making sure you listen."

"With boycott? No solve problem, only make worse—"

"We already got your attention, don't we? Now we have to turn a few more heads."

Mr. Rhee was silent. He stared at them, then turned slowly, walking back to the store, his steps heavy.

Mrs. Rhee asked him questions in Korean, and he answered tersely. He then said to Tom, "They don't listen." He rubbed his eyes.

A young woman on her way to work passed the group outside, glancing at the protestors. One person unrolling a banner said, "Boycott this store." But the woman ignored him and walked in. Tom moved back to the register, and Mr. Rhee went to the telephone. After about ten minutes, the chants began, the same as yesterday, though there were more voices, and Tom tried to act as if the streets were silent—no chants, no voices, no small speeches. The slogans still floated into the store, however, and Tom checked outside every so often, finding their numbers growing slowly.

By noon, there were more than a dozen. Mr. Rhee was making a few more calls, his voice low and secretive. Tom was working behind the register for the beginning of the lunch crowd, and within a half hour, the store was busy. The boycott didn't seem to be having much effect on the customers other than arousing some curiosity. Mr. Rhee checked his watch, then waited outside while Mrs. Rhee came out from the back room and looked through the window every few minutes.

While he was ringing up a customer he heard the chants getting louder and angrier. The noise entered the store and turned customers' heads. Then, a crowd of people formed at the doorway, gathering around Mr. Rhee. They followed him inside. Jeers came from the protestors, and about a dozen people of different races, sexes, and ages walked in, talking among themselves, and they lined up to buy small things—cigarettes, gum, a lottery ticket. One grey-haired man in this group bought some mints and gave Tom a wink. Tom asked what

was going on, and the man looked at him with surprise, telling him, "Boycott breakers." The protestors
were booing, hissing, calling out, "You're supporting racism!" and "Boycott!" but the noise level in the
store was drowning out the disorganized chants.
Mrs. Rhee took over the register as Tom looked outside. The protestors were watching the doorway,
arguing among themselves, pointing inside. They
tried different chants, stopped, and began again.

In the store Tom heard different snippets
of conversation as he walked back to the register. Nip
this in the bud, breaking their spirit, playing their
game, Brooklyn boycott.

But after a few minutes, there were more
voices outside. The chants grew louder and the people
in the store turned to see. Someone groaned. Another voice said, "The media." Some of the customers
filed out to look, and Tom left the register. Two news
vans, different networks, were double-parked along
the street, satellite dishes on the top of their roofs.
Near the white van a woman with her hair tied
tightly back was pointing a cameraman and a sound
man to the store. In the blue van, a man who looked
vaguely familiar was climbing out of the passenger
side, fixing his jacket. Tom watched the protestors
chanting with more energy. Mrs. Rhee called him
back to the register.

While he was working, a bright light

entered the store—a spotlight. A cameraman was pointing his camera inside. The man swept it across the store, ending with Tom. The light stayed on him. He turned away. "No camera in store," Mr. Rhee said, putting his hand in front of the lens. The cameraman pulled back, and the bright light disappeared, the store suddenly dark. The woman interviewed Mr. Rhee outside. His voice was calm, deliberate. The chanting continued in the background.

By one-thirty, most of the customers were gone, but the sidewalk was crowded with people who had seen the cars and cameras. Mr. Rhee had to leave for New Jersey, though he was reluctant. Mrs. Rhee talked to him in Korean, trying to convince him. He approached Tom. "I be back at six," he said.

"What's going to happen?" Tom asked, motioning outside.

"Before TV news come, we okay, but now...I don't know." He moved closer to Tom. "Take care of store, okay?"

Tom nodded and watched him leave, walking by the protestors, who were taking a break. They ignored him. Sitting on the curb and eating, they had stacked their picket signs on the sidewalk and were talking. Tom noticed the man and woman from yesterday and this morning were not here. In fact, most of the faces were unfamiliar. Were they doing this in shifts?

It was a slow afternoon, and only a few customers came in. By five, the protestors had packed and were leaving. Mrs. Rhee visibly relaxed, the squinting, worrying look leaving her face as the last car drove off. She turned to Tom and said, "Maybe they don't come back tomorrow."

He told her he hoped not.

Mrs. Rhee took over the register for the rush-hour crowd and Tom sat outside by the fruit, glad that the protestors were gone and really hoping, like Mrs. Rhee, that they'd get tired of this. When he saw June walking down the street towards him, he didn't at first recognize her, thinking it was someone who looked like her, but then she waved and smiled, and he stood up off the stool.

"You're here," he said. "Didn't you go to school today?"

She shook her head. "I hung out. I was getting tired of that place."

"What're your parents going to say?"

"Nothing, since they won't know."

Mrs. Rhee must have heard her, because she called out in Korean.

"One sec," June called out. To Tom she whispered, "Hey how about tonight? Pizza?"

Tom checked to see if the Mrs. Rhee was nearby.

"You know that pizza place a few blocks

down?" she asked. "Meet you there at seven?"

He nodded as she walked inside and said hello to her mother.

Later, when Mr. Rhee returned to the store, he asked Tom if anything had happened while he had been gone, and he was relieved when Tom told him no. But when Tom mentioned that business was a little slow, Mr. Rhee stared at the ground.

"We have to see," he said to Tom. He went inside to talk to his wife.

Δ

At the pizza parlor, Tom waited at the table by the front window, sipping a soda. He didn't care anymore—he'd have dinner with June and take it from there. With all this going on, what did it matter that he was with her? Besides, he felt he had to talk to someone about all this, if only to figure out what to do next, if anything. He felt that the Rhees blamed him, and wasn't sure if he should do something, because what if the boycotters wanted him fired? What if the Rhees saw this as their only course of action? Then what would he do?

June walked in fifteen minutes late, and sat down next to him, crossing her legs. She leaned back and said, "Well, it looks like things are getting worse."

Tom didn't say anything.

"But there's not much they can do," she

said. "They're talking to a lawyer for the Korean Grocery Association, but besides that, they have to just wait and see."

"They blame me, don't they," he said, feeling heavier.

"They haven't said anything like that."

"You know, I didn't *mean* to do anything to them. And Christ, this was bound to happen sooner or later."

"I know, Tom," she said. "Let's not talk about it right now." She stared out the window. "Hey, there's Mr. Harris."

Tom turned and saw the slightly stooped-over figure of Mr. Harris walking across the street. Tom stiffened. "Turn away," he said. "Don't let him see us."

"What?"

"Mr. Harris," Tom said, turning his back to the window. "What if he sees us and tells your parents?"

"Don't worry, he can't see us."

"He might. Stop looking that way."

She shook her head. "Don't worry about it."

Tom became annoyed. "You think your parents will like our spending so much time together?"

"You worry too much, you know that?"

she said, staring at him. "Just take it easy." She stood up. "I'm going to get something, you want a slice?"

"No thanks." He just hadn't been feeling very hungry lately. While she walked to the counter, he played with his ice, thinking about what she had said. She was being careless and didn't seem to care if they jeopardized his job. What'd she have worry about? She had parents who'd take care of her. He watched June take out some loose bills and pay the cashier—she stood on her toes even though she didn't have to, and the muscles in her calves rose and bunched together, some tendons striated down the sides of her legs. She must walk often, or maybe she ran, though she seemed slightly heavy for a runner.

She returned and said, "Too bad I missed the excitement."

"You mean the TV people?"

"That and the boycotters."

Tom then realized that the news story might air tonight. He mentioned this to her and she brightened.

"That's right," she said, sitting down. "We've got to see it."

While she ate and they talked about the day's events, Tom watched her pick at her pizza, pulling off small chunks and nibbling at them. He watched her lips while she spoke. She was telling him about wanting to quit summer school but being afraid of telling her parents this. It made him feel old, listening to her talk about school and parents.

They walked back to his apartment and began watching TV, flipping through the channels for the news. They couldn't find any, so he left the set on and turned down the volume. She leaned back against the wall and crossed her legs and her ankles. "What do you plan to do once this blows over?" she asked.

"What?"

"After all this dies down. It will. But what do you want to do?"

"Do? I don't know. What do you want to do?"

"I want to go to college, then law school."

"That's great," he said, suddenly feeling tired.

"But what about you? Don't you want to do something?"

Tom thought about this. Do what? He just couldn't seem to care. "Not right now. I just want to have enough money for food, rent, and whatever."

"But what about the future? Don't you want a career, a family, or something?"

He paused. "Not really."

June stared at him for a while. "You're kind of strange, Tom."

He didn't know how to answer that, and

simply shrugged.

"Oh," she said, pointing to the TV. "The news."

He turned up the volume and sat next to her on the mattress, their hips touching, their bodies against the wall. The newscaster began going through the stories of the day, but instead of paying attention, he began drifting. The voices of the news droned and floated in and out of his thoughts—thoughts of the day, of June, of why he didn't have that future-oriented thinking that June had. He had always been like this, and maybe that was the problem.

The words "Korean Grocery" jarred him, and June poked him with her elbow. He sat up.

Racial tensions boil over this summer, the newscaster said.

She began talking about the previous boycott in Brooklyn, which was getting the most media attention, but which was only one of a few around the country. She spoke of Chicago and California, and of other incidents in the tri-state area. *The boycott of the Fruit 'N Food Grocery in Kasdan, Queens also continues today,* she said.

Leaning closer to the screen, he saw a panning shot of the protestors. A voice-over of another reporter came on, and Tom stared at the images, amazed to see them on television. He had seen these same things this afternoon. It seemed unreal.

Apparently sparked by a cashier pulling a gun on a suspected shoplifter, the Fruit 'N Food boycott began yesterday morning, and protestors vow to continue until their voices are heard.

The people on camera were pumping their signs and waving their banners. Tom was mesmerized. For some reason, it looked like there were more protestors than there actually had been. Maybe it was the camera angle, or the slow, sweeping shot, but instead of the dozen or so protestors, no more than fifteen by the end of the day, it appeared as if there had been twice or even three times that many.

"Hey," June said.

African-Americans here contend that the Korean grocers are inconsiderate of and even hostile to them because of their skin color.

The screen cut to two elderly black women, standing together. The reporter asked them a question but Tom didn't hear it clearly because he suddenly recognized these two women. They had come to the store often. They dressed alike, and usually bought similar things. But he didn't remember seeing them with the other protestors.

Just because we black don't mean we bad customers, one of them said.

They slap the change at us, and are so rude, the other added.

Mr. Rhee was then in the center of the

screen, the microphone being held at his face by the reporter. Mr. Rhee said something about working together and talking about this to stop the problems. He looked so tired with the bags under his eyes, the harsh light revealing the wrinkles along his mouth and forehead. He spoke calmly, but his eyes showed his anxiety. The camera cut to the inside of the store, and Tom saw the line of customers at the register, and he saw himself. He was looking at the purchases and ringing up the prices. How strange. Was this what he looked like? He was so skinny, gaunt, and his hair was much longer than he had thought. Tom watched himself look at the camera for a full second, then turn away. Had he stared that long? It hadn't seemed like it at the time. He thought he had just glanced at the camera, but it had actually been for a long time. Maybe he had been thinking of something else and hadn't noticed the camera, or maybe things happened slower than he thought. The time in his head and real time seemed so different. Everything happened slower in the real world.

Tom stared at the commercials for a few seconds until June shook her head. "Hey. It looks bad."

He agreed. Had he been "inconsiderate" towards the customers? Was he racist?

"So you were on TV. You're famous," she said, breaking into his thoughts. "This is so

142

weird."

"Great," he said, worried about the story. This meant it would get bigger.

"I've never been on TV," she said. "Never been anywhere."

He was silent for a minute, then told her about the time he had been in the newspaper once— the front page of the *Times'* Metropolitan section. It was a shot of his fifth grade class at the Museum of Natural History, and he remembered it being posted on the board in his classroom on the day the paper came out. It had stayed up there all year. The picture was of his class trip, and the only thing he remembered of that day were the fake cavemen behind the glass display, in their natural environment. His face had not come out clearly.

"Did your parents see it?" she asked.

"My father?" he said. "He might have, but I don't know. I didn't see him that much."

"Why not?"

Tom stood up, then went to the kitchen area to get some water. "He worked and didn't come home until late."

"A latch-key kid," she said.

Tom said yes. She turned the TV down. He checked his watch, and June noticed this.

"You know, maybe I ought to let you rest tonight," she said. "I can take a cab to my friend's place. She won't mind."

Tom nodded, but wasn't sure if he wanted her to go. "If you want to," he said. He sipped warm tap water from his cup, and returned to her, sitting on the edge of the mattress, by her head, and watching the small TV screen, the figures no larger than his hand, black and white static-filled images moving back and forth in that small space. He reached over and changed the channel to find some more news, and then watched a newscaster sit in front of him and talk silently to him. So he had made the news. Now everyone knew about the boycotts. He became uneasy at the thought of this.

When he glanced at June he was startled to see her with her eyes closed, her mouth slightly open. "June?" he whispered.

She breathed deeply.

Should he wake her? No, he should let her sleep. Someone should get some sleep around here. He went to his window and sat on the sill, watching her. She was sleeping while he had insomnia. Somehow all this made perfect sense. He was glad he wouldn't have to be alone tonight.

TEN

Mr. Rhee told Tom that he was staying at the store today, despite the number of things he still had to do in New Jersey. He would try to get to those later, since the protests worried him and he didn't want to leave the store with just Tom and Mrs. Rhee. They were surprised to find the protestors setting up already.

"They're early," Tom said to Mr. Rhee as he walked outside with his apron on.

"The news will bring more people."

Tom said he had seen it.

Mr. Rhee looked at him, and nodded.

It was mid-morning and there were about ten people on the sidewalk curb and street in front. Less than twenty feet away from the fruit stand, the protestors made Tom uncomfortable with their silence, their stares. He could feel the new tension, the new mood, not just in him or in the Rhees, but in the people across from him. They were bent over their signs with markers, spray paint, and staplers, slowly and carefully drawing their letters of protest, their charges of racism, their calls to boycott, and in the warm morning air with their foreheads already sweating from the work, only a few quiet words were exchanged between them. They didn't laugh or smile or display anything except their grim purpose.

Tom thought about June still sleeping when he had left this morning. For most of the night he had watched her sleep, him sitting on the windowsill or on the floor by the TV, and she, rolling back and forth uncomfortably, tugging at her clothes, smacking her lips. He had tried to wake her before he had left, telling her she might miss school, but she had said she was skipping it again and she promptly went back to sleep. He had left a note asking her to lock up before she left. She had looked pretty last night while her tangled hair fell over her face and every so often she would mumble something unintelligible. Staying up all night wasn't so bad with her around, even if she was asleep, since the company somehow made it easier.

At eleven, Tom helped Mr. Rhee record the new shipment of the Asian Vegetables, the China Peas, Bok Choy, Bean Sprouts, Nappa Cabbage, and Japanese Eggplants. Mrs. Rhee was at the register, and although the protestors were ready—their signs were finished—they hadn't yet begun their chants.

There were now almost twenty people in front of the store, talking quietly. Mrs. Rhee checked on them periodically. She touched her index finger to her lower lip and stared. Mr. Rhee paced the back room, looking out whenever a customer walked in, ringing the front bell. Tom unloaded more crates and marked his invoice. He watched Mr. Rhee's movements from the corner of his eye. Mr. Rhee couldn't keep still.

"Worried?" Tom asked.

"I hope they don't scare customer away."

The bell went off again. Tom looked out with Mr. Rhee and about six or seven customers came in. Why were the protestors silent?

Mr. Rhee walked out and spoke to his wife. She said something and shook her head. Tom went to the front entrance and tried to see what the protestors were doing. Now, there were about twenty-five, maybe more. "They seem to be waiting for more people," he told Mr. Rhee.

"More," Mr. Rhee repeated to himself.

Some customers came into the store confused, glancing back at the crowd outside. They asked Mrs. Rhee about it, but she shrugged it off.

Then, at noon, there were loud voices outside. Mrs. Rhee rushed to look and she waved for Mr. Rhee to come. He hurried to her, weaving around customers. After watching them from the back room, Tom followed.

The crowd had grown to thirty, and there was a man talking to them all. They were listening intently, ignoring the curious stares of bystanders. The man was wearing jeans and a brown suede jacket. He looked middle-aged, with slightly greying hair on the sides of his afro, and he was slim, athletic.

A customer approached and Tom went back to work, moving to the back room, but as he sat down he heard a loud, short burst of sound, like a siren cut short. *Eee-op.* And again, the short siren filled the store. Mr. Rhee jumped. Then, static and a voice. "Testing, testing."

They looked out and the man was standing on an upside down garbage can; he was holding a bullhorn. "Can you hear me?" he asked, his voice filling the street.

The crowd answered yes.

The man began to speak but some feedback screeched through the bullhorn. He tried it again. "Can everyone hear me?"

"Yes," they answered.

"Can *you* hear me?" he asked, turning to the store. The crowd laughed. Tom and Mrs. Rhee withdrew into the store, hiding. Tom felt his neck getting warmer. Mr. Rhee cursed under his breath. Mrs. Rhee asked him something in Korean. He shook his head.

"I sure hope they're listening," the man

said. "Since this is all for their benefit." His metallic voice seemed to vibrate the windows.

More laughter.

"They best be listening, 'cause we sure ain't leaving until they do!"

Clapping, cheering.

Mr. Rhee stormed to the back room, and picked up the phone. Tom asked Mrs. Rhee who he was calling.

"Police."

The man with the bullhorn continued to talk and it was difficult to ignore him—his voice was everywhere. Tom tried to block him out. Mrs. Rhee closed the front door tightly, which helped a little.

...can't close the door to our grievances. We are tired of the racism, of the prejudice....

Tom began to reprice some soup cans using the label gun. The French Onion with Beef Stock came first: $ .99. Cream of Chicken: $ .66. He began stamping, listening to the double clicking of the gun.

...the African-American is being bled dry....

Clickclick: $ .75. Clickclick: $ .69. He found a rhythm that he enjoyed and concentrated on hitting the top of the cans in the center. Bulls-eye.

...taking our money, our business opportunity —opportunity that the white man denies us —and treating us like we are worse than them!

Next came the canned vegetables. String beans. Corn. Peas. He changed the numbers on the stamp and began pricing these.

...so we're going to do what?

Boycott!

The chanting began and Tom listened for a second. He looked through the store window and saw that the crowd was growing, and people all along the street were watching the protest. Someone with a camera was moving around the group, photographing them. Another person held up a tape recorder to them. Tom went back to work.

When the police car arrived, Mr. Rhee went outside amidst the boos and hisses aimed first at the police then at Mr. Rhee himself. They yelled out names. "Racist!" a few of them yelled together. Mr. Rhee ignored them and met the two uniformed police officers—different from the last time; they were both white—in front of the store. They talked, their words drowned out by the chanting and yelling. The younger office with curly brown hair looked at Mrs. Rhee and Tom standing in the doorway, and nodded to them. Mr. Rhee was motioning to the protestors then to the store. The older policeman, who was balding, shook his head and pointed to the group.

A teenager down the street walking towards the store, saw the protestors, the police, and turned around. Tom checked if Mrs. Rhee had seen this. She hadn't. Her eyes were locked on the policeman. Tom heard bits of their conversation. As long as the protestors didn't interfere with the traffic in and out of the store, and stayed on public property, they were within their rights to protest.

Mr. Rhee pointed to his ear and said something about the noise. The policeman shook his head and said something. They finished talking and Mr. Rhee watched the officers return to their patrol car. The protestors cheered. He then spoke to his wife in Korean and she raised her voice, pointing to the departing car. Mr. Rhee said, "Like last time. They can't do anything yet." They continued talking and Tom returned to the back room.

By two, the crowd had grown to forty, gathering along the sidewalk and street, and there were six or seven reporters and photographers, and one television camera. There were only three customers in the store, and any customer could see and hear the commotion from blocks away. If the presence of this crowd didn't deter the customer, the jeers and taunts by the protestors would.

Tom had a tremendous headache from the chanting and the bullhorn siren which they let off every ten minutes. The sun was bright, the day getting hotter, and he saw many of the protestors taking off their jackets, going for drinks, wiping their faces.

After Tom finished most of his work, he asked Mr. Rhee if he could take a break. He wanted to take a walk, get away from the noise. Mr. Rhee agreed, looking around the store. Two customers. Tom hung his apron and went outside, hit by a wall of heat and noise. They started yelling louder as he left the store. "Here come one of them now!" someone said. "Greedy Korean!" "Racist!" "Go back home to Korea!" "He think we dumb niggers!"

He stopped for a second, and looked at them. To him their faces were contorted with anger, veins bulging in their necks from shouting, teeth gritting. They were sweating in the sun, beads dripping. Some were raising their fists, others pointing as they cursed him. They hated him. They didn't even know him, but they hated him. He shook his head and continued. They became louder. Then, a large paper cup landed at his feet, splashing soda and ice over his pants and shoes. The thin plastic cover rolled across the sidewalk, the ice scattered in front of him, sparkling in the light. Tom stopped, feeling the wetness, and turned. They taunted him: "Come on, fucker! *Do* something, mother-fucker!" Some were still yelling "Boycott!" A confusing mixture of chants and curses swarmed around him. "Come on, *try* something!"

He stared at them. The soda was soaking through; he felt it on his leg, in his sock. They were still yelling, their chants blending together into a wave of indistinguishable noises. The harsh sounds rising and falling in his head, a rumbling followed by a building crescendo of screams and curses and chants until it exploded at its zenith and fell apart into disconnected voices. He closed his eyes and held his head. He couldn't block it out. He stumbled away from the store, touching the window, then the brick, when something hit him on his T-shirt and fell to the ground, frightening him. He looked down. A piece of hamburger. Ketchup stains over his chest. They laughed. "The boy's bleedin'! He got shot!" More laughed. Something else slapped into his neck. A doughnut. Tom felt the remains of it oozing down his shirt. Without thinking he whirled around and called them assholes. One of the men called him a fucking chinko and pushed forward through the protestors. Someone held him back. Hold up hold up, someone said. Not yet.

Another cup of something was thrown at Tom, but he ducked and a styrofoam cup splashed black liquid onto the brick wall, getting some on his cheek. Warm coffee. He walked down the street, ignoring the jeers and laughs. When he turned the corner he saw that they were throwing more things at the store. Objects too small for him to distinguish arced over the sidewalk and splashed onto the fruit stands and the front window. Mrs. Rhee opened the front door and screamed something at them but they didn't stop. Tom turned away and continued walking. His eyes were blurry, his head throbbing, and he felt his heart slamming in his chest. Instead of walking around the block to cool off, like he had planned to, he walked home and didn't stop.

Δ

When Tom arrived, angry thoughts still flying through his head, he threw open the door and was surprised to see June still on his mattress, wrapped in his sheets. Her jeans and shoes were in a pile next to her. She lifted her head slowly, blinking.

"Hey," she said. She propped herself up on her elbows. "What happened to you?"

Tom turned and kicked the coffee table violently, sending it crashing across the floor. June jumped up. He looked at his ketchup stained shirt, the red and brown coagulating, and his pants soaked with soda, and he cursed. He said, "The goddamn protestors did this." He walked quickly to the shower, taking off his clothes as he entered the bathroom. He heard June get up.

As he climbed into the shower, he thought, They made me look like a fool. "Assholes!" he said, turning the hot water up, spraying his face. He soaped himself quickly and washed off the sticky soda from his legs. June knocked at the open bathroom door.

"Yeah?" he said.

"You all right?" she asked. "Can I come in?"

"How come you're not at school again?" he asked, annoyed.

"I'm just so sick of it. Maybe I'll just drop out. It's only summer school."

He heard her at the sink, washing up. "Those protestors are just angry," she said. "They want to make trouble."

"To hell with them." He let the water beat the back of his neck and he began to feel better.

"Can I borrow your toothbrush?" she asked.

He said yes and listened to her running the faucet and then brushing her teeth. At that moment he suddenly felt like he was married, as if this was a typical morning for them, and he stood still in the shower, confused. He heard June spit into the sink, gargle, and then leave the bathroom. Husband and wife. This appealed to him. He finished his shower and grabbed the towel hanging on the wall, drying himself quickly.

"I guess I'll go back with you," June said as he came out buttoning his jeans and pulling on a new shirt. She had dressed, and was putting her hair in an elastic band with ruffles.

"What are you going to tell your parents?"

She shrugged.

"Okay, let's go." They left the apartment and walked in silence.

When they were a block away from the store, they heard the dim chants growing louder. June said, "Sounds bigger."

"It is."

They soon saw the crowd spilling over the streets, the numbers at least a hundred, and Tom was not surprised to see two police cars nearby. As they neared the store, Tom turned to her and said, "Maybe we shouldn't go in together."

"What? Oh," she said. "No, it doesn't matter. I'll just say I saw you on your way here. Don't worry." She looked towards the front of the store and pointed. The front window was broken, shards of glass sticking out from a gaping hole in the center. They walked in, the crowd booing and cursing them, and saw two policemen in the empty store, talking to the Rhees.

"Arrest them! They get violent! They break window!" Mrs. Rhee yelled, her voice rising above the protestors.

The policemen and the Rhees turned to Tom and June as they walked in, the noise outside rising. The Rhees looked harder at June, surprised by her presence—Mr. Rhee looked back at Tom and then at June again. One officer began saying something about being careful and they had to think of public safety. Tom looked back outside and saw that the protestors were pumping their fists with the chants, and they all seemed to be looking directly at him. Mr. Rhee went to the back room to make a telephone call.

When the police left the store, the cheering and chanting rose for an instant, then returned to its rhythmic "Boycott this store," the syncopated one-two-three, Boy-cott-thisstore, Boy-cott-thisstore. Mr. Rhee came back from the telephone and he began talking to his wife in Korean. Soon, they were arguing while Tom stood behind the register, waiting for customers that didn't come. How long could this last?

Mr. Rhee raised his voice for an instant, then waved his hand and walked into the back room, and he spoke with June. Mrs. Rhee turned to stare out at the protestors. She walked to Tom.

"Mr. Rhee want to close store now."

"Now?"

"We close now, then we show they right, and we lose. We should stay open, then we show that we not give up."

He nodded. "What happened to the window?" he asked, pointing to the jagged pieces of glass hanging dangerously.

"Man who threw rock, he ran away. Police don't catch."

Then, there was a loud crash, and Tom and Mrs. Rhee hurried to the front door. A man was kicking the stand over. The crowd erupted with cheers. "Put them out of business!" someone yelled.

Before Tom or Mrs. Rhee had a chance to react, two policemen rushed over to the man and shoved him against the wall, wrenching his arm up behind his back, searching him, and then handcuffing him. The crowd booed and called the police "pigs" and "racists". One of the policemen hurried back to the patrol car and used the radio. The other policeman walked the smiling protestor to the car at a slower pace. The steel handcuffs on his wrists glinted in the sun. They drove off, leaving only one patrol car double parked two stores down.

Tom and the Rhees went out to collect the fruit and fix the stand. The protestors began cursing them. "Go fucking home, chinks!" "You don't belong here!" "Go fucking back to Korea!" Tom tried to ignore them but he felt his head pounding and his eyes blurring with anger, listening to these taunts which he hadn't heard since he was a child. Only twenty or so feet of sidewalk separated them, and he could see the chalk line they had drawn on the ground—their boundaries—disappear under their shoes with each new chant. They inched forward, then drew back. Forward and back. Forward and back. Tom tried not to look at them, but they kept hurling curses.

"Thomas, you go back inside," Mrs. Rhee said, watching him carefully.

He glanced at Mr. Rhee, who was putting the fallen fruit in a crate, and at June, who was helping her father but was also watching Tom. He nodded to Mrs. Rhee, stood, and walked back inside. He noticed that there were still some small pieces of glass on the floor, so he began sweeping this, trying to ignore the jeers coming through the hole.

Δ

Later that evening, Tom went to meet June at a small bar, The Ruby Inn, a few blocks further south from Tom's apartment. Even though it was Friday, June had told her parents that she wanted to stay over at her friend's place again, and they, her parents, were too preoccupied to ask questions. Tom had arrived at the bar first, and had a beer while he thought about himself and Mr. Rhee fixing that window—they had nailed some plywood over it, which cut off some light and made the store seem like it was underground. It also made the protestors seem farther away, out of sight, and the disembodied chants suddenly had become less real.

Tom looked around the bar. It was almost empty with two couples at a table and a few people at the bar stools, a low murmur mingling with the TV on the wall near Tom; a commercial was playing and no one paid attention to it. It was an old, large color television mounted on the wall, and Tom, wanting to change the channel, stood and checked if anyone would mind. No one noticed him. He flipped the big dial until he found the news. Then, ordering another beer, he sat down and waited for June. As he expected, the boycott story soon came on.

The Korean grocery boycott heated up today, the newscaster said. *A crowd of approximately two hundred protested the Fruit 'N Food grocery in Kasdan, Queens. This is the third day of this demonstration, and organizers say they hope to shut down the store and put the owners out of business.*

The screen cut to the demonstrations, the same scenes Tom had watched earlier, and the voice-over reviewed the past three days. Tom sipped his beer, watching the crowds pump their signs and chant into the cameras and listening to the recap of last night's story. He glanced around him and saw that no one was paying attention to the news. For the other customers, this was just another boring newscast even though this had happened a few blocks up the road.

Today, police arrested one demonstrator for knocking over the fruit stands, the voice-over continued. *The suspect, a young African-American man whose name hasn't been released, was charged with disorderly conduct and was fined and released shortly afterwards.* The story ended with a note that the attorneys for the Korean Grocery Association of New York were filing for emergency injunctive relief because of the effects the protests were having on the store owners' business. This strategy was used in the Brooklyn boycotts to bring in more police protection.

The next news story, a profile of similar racial tensions in Los Angeles, came on but Tom only half-listened. He told himself that this wasn't as bad as it seemed. Funny, the newscaster hadn't said anything about the broken window. He shrugged. The less said about the violence, the better. No need to give people ideas.

When June finally arrived, a half hour late, she stopped at the front entrance and searched the room. When she saw Tom she brightened, and weaved around the tables and chairs. She apologized as soon as she sat down. "My parents were giving me a hard time about skipping school today."

"Did they know where you were?"

She shook her head. "But I think they were a little suspicious when we came in together."

"I knew it," Tom said. He closed his eyes for a second, and inhaled deeply. "What else did they say?" He was slightly annoyed at her now, since he had wanted to be more careful.

"I wouldn't worry about it," she said.

"They're just going nuts over the boycott thing. They don't want to default on any loans."

"Is that going to happen?"

"It might," she said. "They don't know yet." She saw his glass mug half-empty with beer. "Can you get me one?"

He nodded and went to the bar, ordering a pitcher and watching June sit back and glance up at the TV. She rested her elbow on the back of her chair and pressed her index finger to her temple, and Tom wasn't sure if she was disturbed by all that had been happening. There was something almost nonchalant about her attitude, and it bothered him. When he brought the beer he asked, "Does any of this—the things at the store—concern you? Aren't you upset?"

She looked surprised. "Of course." But then she tilted her head to the side, thinking. She sighed. "But not as much as my parents. I don't know, somehow a lot of this doesn't seem real. Even though I see it all, it's like, I'm just watching it happen, but it's not real."

"But it's your family, your family's business."

"I know, I know," she said, nodding quickly. "Don't you think I know that?" She poured herself a tall glass of beer and drank some of it. She stared at her glass. "I'll tell you something, and I know you'll think it's terrible," she said. "But when all this was beginning, the only thing I thought was, 'Who'll pay for my college education if this store goes under?'"

Tom looked at her with surprise.

"I know it's bad, but I think my parents have drilled this into me so much that that's all I can think about. Education. Career. Money." She shook her head. "You don't think like that. Maybe that's better."

Tom sensed a criticism, especially once he remembered what she had said about him not thinking about his future. He frowned, unsure if he should reply.

"No, it's a good thing sometimes, not to be so uptight," she said, glancing at him.

"I wish you'd stop that."

She laughed quietly. "You don't have to get like that. I was saying that I like you. That's all."

Tom nodded uncomfortably.

Δ

In his apartment, June lay on the mattress and fell asleep almost immediately, the beers making them both slightly drunk, but nothing like that night they had first gone out. Tonight, Tom felt lightheaded and slightly numb, staring at June's tired body next to him as she opened her eyes and asked him if he minded that she crashed. Tom said no, he didn't mind, and saw her eyelids close as she smiled quickly, and within minutes, she was asleep. Yet he kept staring at her. The reality of the situation, that he was in bed with a sixteen-year-old, that he was having sex with a kid really, struck him, and he became disgusted with himself. What was he thinking? He could get arrested for this, all because he was lonely? He stood up and turned on the TV, sitting on the floor and searching for the news. He had to watch the coverage of the boycott over and over again, even if it was, in some cases, the exact same report.

He turned to June, whose body was still, and thought about breaking it off with her somehow. He liked her, and when she was around, even now as she slept, he felt more comfortable, but he knew this wasn't right. He turned back to the TV, not wanting to think about it.

The news report he had heard earlier came on, commenting on the disorderly conduct arrest. He watched it again.

Then, the report went further. *And, this late-breaking bulletin: Responding to an anonymous tip regarding a possible bomb threat, police officers discovered gasoline bombs on the roof of a check-cashing business. The building is directly across from the Fruit 'N Food grocery.*

Tom jumped forward and turned the sound up. June stirred. The camera cut close to the Checks Cashed building at night, the neon sign lighting up the front window.

At nine-thirty this evening, police received a phone call from someone who gave an address and claimed that there might be some bombs up on the roof. When conducting a sweep of the building, police officers found a dozen gasoline bombs, known as Molotov Cocktails. They immediately radioed the bomb squad who promptly disposed of the potentially devastating home-made fire bombs.

The camera then showed a police officer, a man with short hair and a mustache. "Sergeant Jameson," the caption read. The reporter asked him about the connection of the bombs with the boycott. The Sergeant replied, "We're not yet sure of the reasons behind this, but because of the proximity to the grocery, there's a chance of a link." There was a sheen of sweat on his forehead under the bright lights, and he wiped it with his hand.

The two anchors came back on the screen and the woman noted that since the beginning of the summer, hate crimes against Asian Americans in New York City had nearly tripled, according to the Bias Investigation Unit of the NYPD. Boycotts like this one were believed to fuel these racially motivated attacks.

The newscasters moved onto another story. Tom turned down the sound. Were these people insane? Gasoline bombs? He couldn't believe that across the street from him had been bombs. Had they been planned for the store?

June mumbled something, then said, "What's going on?" in a cracked voice.

"Nothing. They found something across the street from the store."

"Oh," she said, and went back to sleep.

He watched her hand twitch for a few seconds, and he pulled the blanket over her.

Δ

Warm blue suffused with cold whiteness, washing over his dreams in a cascade of falling shades, darkening him and comforting him. He woke up sweaty, shivering, but it didn't seem as bad as other nights. He rolled over and huddled closer to June, who then shifted and wrapped an arm around him. He fell back asleep.

ELEVEN

The next time Tom opened his eyes the morning sun was lighting up the room. He had had a few good hours of sleep, but he wasn't refreshed. He felt dirty and tired and irritable. His body ached and his mouth was parched. A slight hangover. He looked at June with annoyance, her mouth open, her cheeks lined with indentations from the sheets, and moved away from her. He was feeling trapped and there wasn't any space left on the mattress for him—he lay curled up at the edge while June sprawled in the center. Checking his watch on the floor, he realized he had awakened too early again, and he knew he wouldn't be able to sleep. He slid onto the floor.

After showering and changing, he paced quietly around the room, restless, impatient, yet he didn't want to wake up June since he didn't feel like talking to her. The room was too small. He had to get out. He left the apartment and began walking up Amber, not caring if he was early. As he crossed the street and dodged a few parked cars, he remembered the news report last night, and his mood darkened. Would they really bomb the grocery? A tiny grocery? Why would they hate it so much that they'd want to set it on fire? He couldn't understand it. Yet he wasn't going to be scared away. This only seemed to strengthen his resolve to be there. Let them do their worst, he thought. Goddamn them all.

When he arrived at the grocery there were dozens of protestors setting up behind the blue wooden police dividers that had the warning "Police Line: Do Not Cross" painted on the sides. Mr. Rhee was talking to a policeman and glanced at Tom as he walked inside. Mrs. Rhee looked up from the register. "Ya, you are early."

"I wanted to help."

She nodded. "We use help. More police come today," she said. "They protect store."

"What can I do?"

"Set up fruit stand. Then take register."

Tom went to work, pulling the stands into place, and carrying the crates of fruit outside. He watched the protestors from the corner of his eye, and they talked among themselves, glancing at the store, at the patrol cars. Mr. Rhee finished talking with the policeman and approached Tom slowly, his clothes wrinkled and his eyes bloodshot.

"How are you?" Mr. Rhee asked.

"I'm okay," Tom said. "There are more police here?"

Mr. Rhee nodded. "Four or five more. And they check building around here. You know why?"

He said he did, and pointed to the Checks Cashed building. "The bombs."

They both stared at the building for a minute.

Tom asked, "What about the New Jersey store?"

Mr. Rhee hesitated. "I don't know. We have to see." He shook his head and walked inside.

About an hour later, the protestors began their chants. The four policeman stood together at the side of the grocery, talking with each other, and occasionally walking into the store, and around the area. As the morning progressed, more and more people began showing up. Tom realized that it was a Saturday, and no one had to work. Although the number of customers had trickled down to a couple every half hour or so, those who did walk in had to deal with the taunts of the protestors. When a black woman walked into the store, people yelled, "Traitor!", "Look at the bitch shop with racists!", "The nigger loves racists!"

The chants continued as Tom rang up the woman, and he could still hear the "nigger" from inside the store. How could they curse her?

"Don't you worry, honey," the woman said to him. "Them ignorant fools gonna get tired soon."

He tried to smile. "Thanks."

When he heard the crowd yell, "Traitor" to someone else, Tom moved back behind the register.

"Go home, old man!"

"Why you d-doing this?" the voice said amidst the jeers. Tom recognized Mr. Harris' voice.

"Whoa ho! Listen to the nigger talk!"

Laughter.

"You is ruining them! Why you d-doing that!"

"Boycott! Boycott!" Their chants drowned him out.

Mr. Harris walked slowly in, wiping his neck with a handkerchief. He saw Tom, raised his hand in a silent "Hello" and moved down the aisle.

Δ

Mr. and Mrs. Rhee were talking for some time in the back room, and Tom wasn't sure what was going on. It was almost eleven, and the chanting outside was giving him a worse headache, so he took some aspirin from the bottle he had put under the counter. Mrs. and Mr. Rhee came out and glanced at him; they both looked worried.

"Thomas, you see Jung-Me today?" Mr. Rhee asked.

Tom's stomach tightened. He wasn't sure if this was a trap. "Why?"

Mrs. Rhee said, "She should be here. It Saturday and we call her friend house. She not go there last night."

Tensing even more, Tom shrugged but felt his face grow hot. The Rhees looked towards the door when the protestors changed their chants, though they didn't seem to be paying attention. Mr. Rhee said something to his wife in Korean, and she shook her head slowly, and answered back. She touched the side of her hair absently, and asked something else. Tom tried to understand what they were saying, but of course couldn't.

"Police?" Mr. Rhee said in English. He shook his head and continued in Korean, motioning to his watch.

"What?" Tom asked. "What'd she say?"

"We wait a little," Mr. Rhee said to Tom. "Maybe she go back home first. Or maybe she forget."

Tom nodded and pretended to clean up the counter, though he watched the Rhees to make sure they weren't going to call the police. The police! He cursed silently. June must still be in his apartment. So goddamn lazy. He should have gotten a phone, but now all he could do was wait. If the Rhees found out she was at his place overnight, they'd fire him, or worse. What would happen if they told the police? This is nuts, he thought, shaking his head in amazement. Could anything happen to him? He pressed his thumb into his forehead, trying to think clearly. What was June's problem? Why didn't she realize this would happen?

For the next hour Mrs. Rhee checked outside every five minutes, surveying the protestors, but also waiting for her daughter. Mr. Rhee used the phone a few times, and Tom listened in, knowing that if Mr. Rhee spoke Korean then he couldn't be calling the police. Tom began to think of a way to leave the store to get her, maybe telling them he needed a break, or that he had forgotten something.

Then Mrs. Rhee said something to Mr. Rhee and they argued for a minute. Mr. Rhee kept shaking his head but Mrs. Rhee was persistent. Finally, Mr. Rhee called to Tom, "What if she get kidnap?"

"Kidnap? I don't think so," he said. "That'd never happen."

Mrs. Rhee folded her arms tightly to her chest. "We don't know. She should be here. Where is she?"

"Maybe we ask police. Maybe they help,"

said Mr. Rhee.

"We tell police outside." Mrs. Rhee began walking towards the door.

"Wait," Tom said, a little too loudly. Mrs. Rhee stopped and looked at him. "I'm sure she'll be back soon" he said. "I wouldn't bother the police yet."

"But where is she?" Mr. Rhee asked "She can be in trouble."

"The *gumdngee* could do something."

Tom said, "Why don't you wait a little longer? That's what the police would say."

They hesitated.

"She probably forgot and went out," Tom added. "She'll be here."

Though they didn't seem satisfied, it was enough to quiet them for now. They returned to work, and Tom began to grow angry at June for making him do this. She was making it harder for everyone. Why was she so careless? Didn't she think? He tried to calm down but he grew more angry at the thought of her sleeping in his bed, in his apartment, making everyone here upset. He knew this had been a mistake, and this just showed that she and he couldn't go out anymore. It was too risky.

When June eventually came in, shortly after lunch, the noise and chanting rising outside, Tom didn't have time to speak to her first. Mrs. Rhee jumped out of the back room when she saw her and said something harsh in Korean.

June looked surprised for a second, but as her mother continued talking, June's face hardened. "What, I'm here now," she said, walking towards her mother. "I had things to do."

Mr. Rhee called her daughter into the back room and June disappeared with her. They closed the door and Tom heard Mr. Rhee raising his voice, almost yelling at her. He heard June's response, also yelling, and Tom sat back in the plastic chair, leaning his head back and closing his eyes. The yelling continued and he listened to the chanting outside, the arguing inside, and he pressed his thumb against his forehead again, wishing all this would end. He couldn't take much more of this. He just couldn't. *It's none of your business!* Tom heard June yell and Mrs. Rhee said something sharp and curt. *Boycott! Boycott!* the chants continued. He felt himself shaking.

The door flew open and June came storming out. Mrs. Rhee said, "Jung-Me!" but June ignored her. "Assholes," she hissed under her breath. She headed for the door.

"Jung-Me!" Mr. Rhee barked. Tom had never heard him like this.

June stopped but didn't turn around.

Mr. Rhee asked her something in Korean.

She said, "I can do what I want." She turned around and added, "I won't be in tonight." Then, to Tom's horror she looked at him and said, "See you later." She hurried out the door, the protestors immediately booing her, curses and chants of "Chink bitch!" and "Racist!" filling the street. Mr. Rhee watched her go, and as soon as the door closed by itself, shutting out some of the sound, his face tightened, and he went back to his wife. The Rhees didn't look at Tom, and he realized that they hadn't heard what she had said to him. After a few seconds, he looked down at his hands and saw that he had been gripping the counter so tightly that his fingertips were white.

Δ

As he suspected, Tom saw June waiting for him when he arrived home. She was sitting on the front steps of the building under the pale yellow light, her hair shining. She was resting her elbows on her knees, and she sat up when she saw him approaching. Though she looked happy to see him and smiled, waved, he was still angry and said as soon as she could hear him, "What the hell did you think you were doing?"

She flinched, and shook her head "What?"

"What were you thinking? You knew

they were expecting you this morning. They were about to call the police!"

"What's your problem?" she asked, standing. "Why are you yelling?" She took a step back and the light fell directly over her head, her face shadowed.

Tom stared at her. "And you almost told them you were coming here. You want me to get fired? Is that it?"

She stiffened. "You mean before? I didn't tell them anything. I just said I was with a friend."

"You told them you weren't going home tonight and then you said you'd see me later."

"What are you talking about? None of this has anything to do with you."

"What if they told the police? What if they found out? Christ, I can get arrested for doing this."

"Is that what you're worried about?"

Tom took a deep breath. "Look, this is getting too risky. I don't like having to lie and cover for you—"

"Cover for me? What the fuck are you talking about?"

"Today! This! I can't take this anymore. I really can't. You're being careless. I just don't need—"

"*You* don't need this. *You* can't take this.

Give me a break, Tom. Just say what's on your mind."

"I am," he said, confused.

"Just say you want to dump me. God, this is great. You fuck me, then you dump me."

"Wait a minute, it's not like that, you know—"

"Bullshit," she said, jutting her jaw out. "Forget it Tom, just forget it." She turned away. "I don't need you."

She kept shaking her head and muttering under her breath. This wasn't happening right. He didn't want it like this; he did this all wrong. "Wait, June...."

She dismissed him with a wave and began walking away.

"I didn't mean it like that."

"You bastard," she said and continued down Amber.

I'm acting like a shit, he thought, but I don't want to stop her; I want her to go. He watched her turn a corner and disappear, her hair swinging up and over her shoulder. He stood there for a while, shocked by what he had just done. But he had no choice! She was acting so stupidly! Finally he said, "Forget her." He didn't want to worry about this, didn't want to think about it. Just go up the your room, lie down and rest, he told himself. Rest. That was what he wanted. Sleep. He thought about the nightmares he was still having and thought, Trapped when I'm awake and asleep.

He entered his apartment and moved through the darkness, June's voice still fresh in his mind. He had no choice—it was getting out of control. She was being careless. He lay on his mattress heavily, and tried to shake the thoughts away.

He closed his eyes and let his mind drift. He suddenly remembered walking through Michaelson Park with his family when his mother was still alive, and this jarred him. He hadn't thought about his mother for so long, especially while in Kasdan. In the memory, everything was still unclear but he saw the remote control sailboats whipping across the small lake in the center of the park, the Reservoir, it was called, though he didn't know if it was still there, and he used to walk along the edge, looking down into the brown murkiness. Kids with kites and frisbees, dogs running freely; he remembered how his mother's moist hand had felt around his, pulling him gently forward, his arm stretching up and his feet dragging because he was looking up at the kites looping back and forth and fluttering with their long tails twirling around and around. He knew he was happy then, and he wondered now, while relaxing back into his pillow, why things went wrong. They always seemed to go wrong. He laughed to himself, thinking, You bastard. June was right. He was a bastard. And he missed her. He liked being with her, and now he felt lousy for letting her walk away.

TWELVE

The same memory of the sailboats fluttering across the Reservoir comes to Tom while in the hospital, the boats changing direction quickly with each new gust of wind; those scenes are so fuzzy, a blurry windowpane between him and the memories. He thinks again about June and remembers feeling sorry for her. He should have realized this would happen. He knows that sending June away like that was a mistake, and understands now where this had to lead. But how could he have known at the time that she'd go back home and, after fighting with her parents and telling them that they don't know anything at all, she would reveal she'd slept with Tom? How could he have foreseen that? It seems so obvious now that with the Rhees' suspicions and June's anger, something would have to have happened, but at that time Tom wasn't thinking of consequences, of logical conclusions. He was thinking of peace, of quiet. He should have known, and now he can envision June that night, right after leaving him, stopping at a pay phone and calling her friend Clara, asking her to come pick her up, but Clara tells her that she shouldn't. June's mother called before, and Clara's mom will call the Rhees as soon as June appears. June can't stay over tonight.

"Shit," is all June can say. She thanks Clara and hangs up. It's all that son of a bitch Tom's fault. He was just using her, leading her on, and she fell for it. How could she have liked him?

She begins walking back to the store, not knowing what she will say to them, but she has no money and will have to go back sooner or later anyway. She approaches the store and sees her parents cleaning up: sweeping the sidewalk and unloading the fruit, locking up the wooden stands. She waits until they are almost done, until her father is pulling down the metal gate over the front of the store and locking it, before she lets them see her. They look up and she sees their relief that she's safe, but they don't say anything. They walk to the car and she follows.

It's an old white Dodge Dart with dents in the front fender from a small accident last year and streaks of mud along the sides. They climb in, and June immediately stares out the window, hoping they leave her alone. Her parents are silent, exhausted from the work day, from the protestors and the police, and her father pumps the gas a few times before he starts the engine, something which annoys her mother since she feels he doesn't have to do that and it seems only to waste gas, but she remains quiet this time. There is no radio—it was stolen two months ago—so they drive in silence towards the Triborough Bridge, the traffic still heavy and the red brake lights of the cars ahead of them filling the car.

"We were worried," June's father finally says in Korean, his voice sounding strangely distant in the low rumble of the engine.

"We almost called the police," her mother says. "You should obey us."

"You don't own me," June says in English. She watches the cars pass them. She thinks, Here they go.

"We are under hardships right now and you are making it worse." Her mother turns around to face her. "Where were you last night?"

"It's none of your business."

"We are your parents!" her mother says, raising her voice. "Everything of you is our business!"

"Leave me alone," June says.

"You are irresponsible. We cannot leave you alone."

"I am not irresponsible."

"You cannot do what you are supposed

to, so you are irresponsible."

"Stop calling me that! You don't know anything. Just get off my back!"

"You were not with Clara, so where did you sleep?" her father asks.

"You'd like to know, wouldn't you," June says.

"And you miss two days of school. We have to pay for that," her mother says.

June thinks about Tom and says, "You don't know anything."

"You are grounded," her mother says. "You will stay home and go only to summer school. If you act like a child, we treat you like one."

"I'm not a child."

Her mother laughs, which angers June even more. "Jung-Me, you are a child and you know nothing yet."

"I'm sixteen! I'm not a kid anymore!"

"Where were you last night?" her father says.

"She is a child," her mother says to her father. "Like a bad-tempered one."

"I was with Tom last night," June finds herself saying, and she can't stop herself, "and I wasn't acting like a child then." She laughs. "You don't know anything."

The sudden silence in the car frightens

her. The tires thump on the concrete in double time, reminding her of a heartbeat. What had she done? It was a mistake! She shouldn't have said anything! The stunned silence continues. She realizes how much trouble she is in when her father says to her mother quietly, in Korean, "I told you."

Δ

The next morning, Tom, on his way to the grocery, wasn't sure if June would show up at work—it was a Sunday—but hoped she wouldn't. He regretted how he had handled her last night, but knew it was for the best. And he had begun thinking about quitting. It just wasn't worth it anymore. When he saw the crowd in front of the store, he became more convinced of this. It was larger than he had ever seen it before; people filled the street and spilled over onto Amber, completely wrapping around the corner and bombarding the Fruit 'N Food on all sides with chants and curses, and it wasn't even ten o'clock yet. He saw the protestors from behind, mostly blacks though he saw Latinos, a few whites, both men and women, even groups of kids. The police were standing to the side, five of them in their blue short-sleeve uniforms and caps, watching the crowd, stonefaced, not talking to one another like they had yesterday. It seemed hotter here, as if all the anger was seeping into the air, filling the streets violently. Tom hesitated, not wanting to approach the crowd that was, to him, frightening. All of them, two hundred or more, against the store, and Tom knew then that this was hopeless. How were the Rhees going to survive this? There were some leaflets scattered on the ground. He picked one up and read it. "Buy Black. Don't support the Koreans who are taking money out of the community. Koreans are racist and treat African-Americans with no respect. BOYCOTT!"

Tom dropped it and walked around the crowd, heading towards the policemen on the sidewalk, making sure they saw him. The crowd suddenly burst out with curses. They called him a chink, a gook, a racist, and the words blended together around him, sinking him, and he tried to ignore them but he just couldn't, and he felt his fists tighten. One of the policemen stepped forward and waved Tom in. A group of protestors began raising and lowering their arms, pointing to Tom in unison, while chanting, "Racist. Racist. Racist." Soon the entire crowd mimicked them, and a low, rumbling chant of "Racist" with a wave of arms aimed towards Tom filled the streets. He hurried past the fruit stand, the boarded-up window, and entered the store.

Mr. and Mrs. Rhee turned to him, and he suddenly sensed something was wrong. They looked at him without smiling, without a greeting, and he thought with fear, *She told them*. His throat tightened and he stopped in the doorway. They stared at him for a second, then went back to work, ignoring him. He was confused. Weren't they going to fire him? Maybe he was imagining this. Maybe June hadn't said anything.

"Morning," he said to Mr. Rhee as he passed him. Mrs. Rhee was bent over a box of cereals, stacking them on a shelf.

Mr. Rhee looked up at Tom, paused, and said, "Good morning, Thomas." He looked quickly away and studied the boxes.

"Is something wrong?" he asked.

"You get to work!" Mrs. Rhee said from the counter, watching them. "No time for talk!"

Tom nodded and went into the back room to get his apron. They know, he thought, feeling their eyes on his back. What the hell.

He stayed in the back room for a while, trying to think of what to do. He peered out into the store and dreaded facing them. June must have told them. But why hadn't they fired him? Why did they still want him to work? He tied his apron on tightly, and took a deep breath. What was he going to do now?

"Thomas! You take register," Mrs. Rhee called to him.

He hurried out and nodded, slipping by her and behind the counter. There were no customers in the store, and he didn't expect any at all today. It was just too intimidating outside. Even now, with the door closed, the chants outside were relentless, and someone was banging on a garbage can, thumping out "Boycott" with the rest of them, a deep bass drum deepening the chants. Tom pressed his palms into his eyes. He thought about having to start looking for another job, and he knew how hard that was around here, so he'd have to move again, and try to find another place to live and work, and even though he had considered this before, the thought weighed heavily on him.

But why didn't they say anything? Mrs. Rhee went into the back room, and Tom watched Mr. Rhee rearrange the shelves, shifting all the goods a few feet to the left. He stood and carried a box to the counter, placing it on the ground.

"Mr. Rhee, is something wrong?" he asked quietly.

Mr. Rhee looked up.

"What's going on?" Tom asked.

Mr. Rhee stared at him for a few seconds, then said, "Last night we talk to June. She tell us about you, about you and her."

Tom nodded, unable to say anything.

"How could you do this to us?" he said. "You older, you should act older."

"I know."

"We let you stay for one more week, then

you have to go."

Tom leaned against the counter and couldn't look him in the eye.

Mr. Rhee shook his head. "Why you do that? We give you job and money and you do this to us."

Mrs. Rhee came out and yelled at Mr. Rhee in Korean.

Mr. Rhee answered back and pointed to Tom. "I tell him already."

She stared at Tom, and then said, "You leave now. No stay for week. You go now!"

Mr. Rhee argued back in Korean, and they began speaking rapidly, interrupting each other and pointing at Tom. Their voices rose and Tom began shaking, hating to hear this yelling and this fighting, and outside the chants seemed to be growing louder as Tom tried to calm down but everything was happening too fast around him. The Rhees' arguing became more heated and he couldn't take this anymore.

"Goddammit!" he yelled. "I'll leave! I'll leave this fucking place, okay?"

"You go now and not come back!" Mrs. Rhee said.

Tom untied his apron and threw it on the ground. "You think I give a shit?" he said, his voice shaking. "You think I give a shit about this goddamn pitiful business? You think I care?" He was shouting now and couldn't stop because this was too much for him and he wouldn't keep this goddamn job now no matter what and who cared about this stupid store and what they thought and if he had screwed up because it just didn't matter anymore.

Mrs. Rhee yelled back, "Get out! Get out now!" Mr. Rhee pulled at her shirt, pulling her away but she rushed straight in front of Tom, yelling in his face, and Tom backed away, feeling her spit on his cheek, and he rushed past her, eyes blurring, and brushed by Mr. Rhee who said something but Tom couldn't hear him now and just wanted to get out of this place. Assholes. He didn't give a shit.

On his way out he accidentally knocked over the snack food stand, the same one that the kid with the bottle had pulled down, and Tom stopped for a second to pick it up but then thought, Who the fuck cares, and continued, pushing the door open with all his strength and it crashed against the doorstop and the bell clanged loudly, the heat and noise almost suffocating Tom. The crowd began yelling at him, calling him a fucker and chanting louder. A black man reached over the blue divider and spit on Tom, a large glob hitting him on the neck and Tom told him to fuck off, to go to hell, and the man called him a fucking chink. Come on, do something, chinko, the man taunted, and Tom stopped walking and gave him the finger slowly, or at least it seemed like it was slowly, with his middle finger almost pointing straight at the man, and he heard one of the policemen call to him, telling him to stand back, but Tom didn't care and called the man a stupid fuck and the man pushed forward, scrapping the wooden divider forward on the pavement, moving past the chalk line, and Tom thought he recognized the man, the one who threw something at him the other day, and Tom called him a stupid dumb fuck again. There was another surge forward, moving towards him, towards the store, one of the dividers moving forward again, getting caught in a crack and slowly falling over, landing on its face with a heavy *ke-thunk* and Tom's eyes met the black man's, and the man jumped forward while the police ran in to stop him, but the entire crowd began moving forward and Tom suddenly felt an explosion on his cheek—someone punching him in the face—and he saw a flash of red and white, and the pain jolted his entire body, and he stumbled backwards, trying to regain his balance, tripping over his own feet and falling to the side, away from the crowd. He saw the police pushing forward, their batons out, and the crowd seemed to roar and fall onto the police, engulfing them. Tom fell back onto the pavement, the breath knocked out of him, hearing a swarm of curses and grunts. Someone screamed and Tom, still stunned from the punch, tried to stand, but his legs were unsteady and someone kicked him in the sides and he screamed out in pain and through watery, stinging eyes he saw a policeman hitting a man, but the crowd jumped on the policeman and punched and kicked him down, and another one turned and ran to his car. Someone kicked Tom again, harder, in his back and he fell against the wall of the store next door, the laundromat, and some men picked up the divider, turned and aimed it towards the grocery store, running with it into the front door, glass crashing down, people cheering. Tom couldn't breathe, the kick having knocked the wind out of him, and he crawled away along the store, watching the people stream into the store, yelling, knocking down the stand, and someone threw something into one of the parked cars, the window shattering. Tom suddenly felt a heavy blow on his neck, everything blurring, and he fell to his knees. Someone kicked him in the head and he felt himself falling dead-weight against the cement, and thought, They're in the store. The Rhees. He lost his strength and passed out.

THIRTEEN

And the Rhees? When Mr. and Mrs. Rhee first heard the yelling they must have hurried to the front door and seen the protestors and the police fighting, the wooden dividers knocked over, fists and clubs and bottles rising and falling into the crowd. Mr. Rhee turned quickly and told Mrs. Rhee to call the police.

"But the police are already here!" she said in Korean.

"Get more!"

She ran to the back room, hearing Mr. Rhee call for Thomas, and she fumbled with the telephone, dropping the handset once and mis-dialing 9-1-1. Her hands were shaking and she couldn't press the small buttons without slipping or missing. She cracked the phone down in frustration and tried again. When she got through she told the operator their address and what was happening. Mrs. Rhee had to keep repeating herself because the operator had trouble understanding her panicked, broken English.

Before she hung up, her husband came running through the door, and pulled her arm hard, hurting her. "Come, we must go!"

But then there was a tremendous shattering of glass, and she jumped. The confusing noise outside filled the store. "What is happening?"

Mr. Rhee looked out, pushed her back into the room and slammed the door, locking it and looking frantically around the room. He pointed to the freezer and said, "Help me push this against the door!"

She tensed, hearing more crashes in the store. Yelling voices.

"Help me!" he cried, struggling with it. She shook off her confusion and they pushed and dragged the freezer to the entrance, the bottom squealing and scratching the cement floor. Mrs. Rhee was getting scared. Everything was too fast, too dizzying.

"What is happening?"

"They are fighting and breaking into the store!"

Crashes, laughing and yelling. Mrs. Rhee felt her stomach drop each time there was another crash. Their store was being destroyed! "We must do something!" she screamed, her voice cracking.

Mr. Rhee jumped to the telephone and

called his friend at the Korean Grocer's Association. Their frantic conversation was periodically interrupted by sounds of something breaking, shattering and crashing. The floor vibrated as something heavy fell. Mrs. Rhee looked desperately around the small cement room, and she felt trapped. There was no way out of the room—no windows, no back doors—except through the store. She then remembered that the money was still in the register and turned abruptly to her husband. "They will get the money!"

He spoke quickly into the phone about calling more help. Something about the police and a riot squad. "*Aigoo,*" he then said, looking at the phone. "*Yubuh seh yo? Yubuh seh yo?*" He hung up and tried to make another call. He said, "It does not work." and gripped the phone in his hand, and turned at his wife, shaking his head. "What can we do?" he asked. The damage in the store continued, more crashes and yelling, and a number of times the back door was rattled and kicked—Mr. Rhee pushed against the freezer to make sure the door was jammed shut. What if those people came in? Mrs. Rhee gripped the edge of the freezer. What if they opened the door?

Δ

You okay? A voice coming from nowhere. *Hey, you got to get up and run. You got to get up.*

Tom slowly awoke, the sounds of breaking glass around him, yelling, laughing, cursing, sirens in the distance. Watery, moving lights around him. Underwater. "What...?" he started to say, blinking, trying to clear his blurry vision, the murkiness around him. A black man crouched over him, nudging his arm.

"You got to get out of here, okay? You okay?" Sweat dripped from the man's face, and he wiped his eyes. He looked quickly behind him, then said to Tom, "You hurt?"

Everything was so sluggish, so...thick. Tom sat up painfully, the man steadying his shoulder, and he saw people across the street crowding by the Checks Cashed store, yelling as two men used a piece of wood to break the heavy glass on the door. More people ran across the street and gathered around the two men. Alarms were going off everywhere. His head throbbed. Tom couldn't think clearly as he tried to orient himself. "What...?"

"You got to go. Get up and run," the man said more urgently.

Tom nodded, getting his bearings. The store. Boycotters "The Rhees," he said, turning. "In the store...." He was shocked to see trampled fruit and broken glass everywhere on the pavement, the wooden stand in pieces, the door broken in dozens of large jagged chunks. He heard people still inside the grocery, crashes and heavy thuds. Yelling. Confusion.

"You hearing me? You got to run." Sirens approaching. The man stood and looked down the street. "Get out of here," he said to Tom, then ran off, moving lightly on his feet and disappearing down a side alley.

People streamed out of the I.D. shop, the front door and window blown out. More sirens. Cheering from the crowd at the Checks Cashed store when the men broke one of the windows on the door. "Get us in," some people cried. Tom heard the man's words *You got to run* and tried to stand, his limbs weak, his head pounding, and noticed that his hands were so cold. The Rhees. Were they okay? He was shaking. Some people running by saw him getting up.

"Get the motherfucker chink!" someone yelled. A few men nearby turned, and moved towards him. They glanced at each other, then at Tom.

Tom stumbled to the side, holding the wall to steady himself, feeling something burn in his sides, then he ran, losing his sense of direction, wanting just to get the hell away. A car alarm went off. He heard the men say something and they began running after him. He felt a surge of panic propel him forward, his legs moving fast and his head jarring with each step, and people on the streets turning to watch him run by. The men behind him were laughing, saying, "Look at the fool go!" When he turned, he saw that they were close behind him, but were barely breathing heavily. They were playing with him. He tried to run faster.

The pain in his sides and in his lungs became unbearable, and he began wheezing, trying to suck in more air. Up ahead, some black kids were watching him and as Tom passed them, one of them jumped forward to trip him. Tom fell over himself, hearing laughter around him, and he saw everything turn and tumble around him. He hit the pavement hard, scraping his palms and forearms. The men behind him yelled and came up to him. One man kicked him in the stomach like a football punter and Tom almost threw up, thinking, I'm going to die. He couldn't breathe and now he wanted to scream out but nothing came.

A crash of shattering glass. An alarm. A crowd of looters rushed into an electronics store and the men around Tom stopped and saw people pouring through a hole in the door, ducking in and punching out more glass. The men immediately ran towards the store, ignoring Tom. People began hurrying out of the store with stereos, VCR's, even small TV's under their arms, as more looters lined by the broken door waiting to jump in amidst the stream of people running out. Yelling. Crashes. Two police cars sped down the street, sirens blaring, and the people scattered. Tom stood up slowly, holding his stomach, and limped down Farrell Street, away from Amber, unable to run now because of the pain, but walking quickly. More sirens in the distance.

On Freemont Avenue, it was quieter. He stopped and rested for a minute, catching his breath. He saw store owners pulling down their security barricades and locking up. In front of a Sports Plus store, a few cars were parked on the sidewalk, blocking the entrance, and a man with a rifle stood by his door. This is insane, Tom thought as he hurried; I could die. Patrol cars sped past Tom, past the Sports Plus, their lights flashing. A store owner called to Tom, "What's going on?" but Tom ignored him and continued walking. A wave of pain spread though his head now, searing him, and he had to hold his stomach and ribs with one arm. He turned on Eisenhower and slowed down, limping and beginning to feel more pain in his knees. He had made it to his building.

In his apartment he locked his door and eased himself on his mattress, shaking, the pain travelling from his head and ribs down to his legs. He couldn't think straight, and kept saying to himself, This is insane, this is insane. He glanced at his door a few times, wondering if anyone could have followed him, and he checked the door again. Locked. Suddenly, he thought of the gun. It was here, somewhere. Where had he left that? Tom began searching the room for it, trying to remember what had happened to it after that night. He could have been killed before, and this shook him. Him killed. Over what? Some goddamned fruit? Some boycott?

More sirens outside. He looked out the window and saw a fire truck going down Amber. Tom turned on the TV, pausing when another wave of pain welled up in the back of his skull. There were special reports on all the channels. He listened while he searched.

...the site of the week-long boycott against the Korean owners. Although the details are still coming in, the looting is apparently a result of tensions between the boycotters and the police who were assigned there to enforce a court order to keep protestors a required distance from the store. Two days ago, when a dozen gasoline bombs were found on the roof of the building across the street, lawyers for the grocery petitioned the Queens County Supreme Court for an emergency injunction. This injunction was granted immediately to balance the protestors' right to congregate and express their views, and the store owner's right to engage in business, and the Court directed the Police to enforce the distance between the store and the boycotters —

Where the fuck was the gun? Tom was shaking and had to sit for a second. Calm down, he told himself. Take it easy. The announcer continued:

Other reports of violence against store owners and some looting are being reported and the NYPD is mobilizing its forces quickly to preempt any further outbreaks. We will keep you posted of any new developments as they come in. The NYPD has advised that people in those areas stay inside as a precautionary measure, although they tell us that they are getting everything under control.

Cold. So cold. None of this is happening. This is crazy. Just get the gun. The Rhees? What if something—

There. Behind the mattress, under the clothes. He held the gun tightly—it was cool and heavy in his hands—and sat against the wall, his knees to his chest, staring at the TV screen, a helicopter's view of Amber Avenue with the dozens of police cars, lights flashing. It looked like people were running away. A fire at one of the stores. Police in riot gear.

Δ

When the sirens began filling the streets, the sounds in the store died down. Mrs. Rhee stood nervously while her husband paced the floor. They were both afraid to come out. More sirens.

"Should we open it?" she asked.

Mr. Rhee stared at her, then nodded. They pushed the freezer away, and listened for a long time, wondering if there were people waiting out there.

"Open it," she said, getting impatient.

He did and when she saw the store, she cried out. She did not expect so much damage: all the shelves were knocked down and broken, the refrigerated displays ripped open, glass everywhere, food and drinks scattered all over the floor, fruits and vegetables crushed and spilling onto the sidewalk and street outside. She could not breathe as she stared at all this. Entire displays knocked over and trampled. Nothing was left standing intact. They were ruined. She knew they could never afford to fix all this. When she looked at the counter, she realized the entire cash register had been stolen, pulled right out of its base. Cartons and packs of cigarettes were trampled on the floor.

Suddenly a bright light filled the store, voices around them. A cameraman walked inside, scaring the Rhees, and a reporter behind the man said, "Excuse me, are you all right—"

Mrs. Rhee looked frantically around her and picked up a can of vegetables and threw it at the camera, hitting the side of it with a cracking sound. The cameraman cursed and ducked.

"Get out! You get out of this store!" Mrs. Rhee yelled, picking up another can and throwing it at the woman.

"But ma'am, we just wanted to—"

"Get out!" She picked up another can

and the two left quickly. Mrs. Rhee was about to throw it at the empty doorway, but she stopped. She looked at the can, wondering if they could salvage any of this, and placed it carefully on the counter, away from the crushed candy. Mr. Rhee looked around the store, and when two policemen came by, Mrs. Rhee went into the back room and let her husband talk to them. She did not want to talk to anyone.

Δ

Getting dark out. Tom sat up and winced as his body seized up in agony. He stopped for a second, then continued. He had to check on them. It was quiet out there, according to the news, and he had to check, just once. Just to make sure. Pain shot again through his body, especially his ribs, and he thought he might have cracked some of them. He winced as he stood up, and his hands were still shaking. I'm dying, he thought; I feel like I'm dying.

He would have to go to the hospital. But he had to make sure they were all right. He had to. He picked up the gun and put it into his pants; the barrel pressed against the base of his spine. He refused to believe that all this was his fault, that they had nothing now because of him. One man could not do all this. But he couldn't think about that right now. All he wanted to do was to check on them.

Outside, Tom heard the alarms going off everywhere. Electronic warbles, sirens, bells echoed in the distance. Most of the stores were closed. He saw some people walking around, but it was quiet out here. When Tom walked north, he saw policemen wearing orange, fluorescent strips over their uniforms directing traffic on Amber, detouring cars away. Beyond the patrol cars was a van that had crashed into a store, the windshields smashed, tires flattened. Another car nearby was blackened with oily soot. Further north were some looted stores with windows smashed, jagged pieces of hanging glass and twisted metal, garbage and debris—food, torn clothing, electronic equipment. Tom avoided the police and continued to walk towards the store in a daze. He smelled smoke and something chemical in the air. Some new clothing littered the sidewalk, the tags still attached, and Tom had to stop and rest every few minutes, his ribs and head hurting too much.

FOURTEEN

Although Tom cannot know precisely what the Rhees did when he wasn't there, especially right before their last meeting, before they would have their final break, he feels compelled to reconstruct their actions to help him understand. He wants to relive it. He tries to see them once they returned from the police station, after the looting and rioting had calmed down. Tom supposes that Mrs. Rhee helped her husband, tired and weakened from this experience, to lift the iron fence to the store, both of them grunting as the gate clattered up into its railings. Together they reinspected the damage, and Tom sees Mrs. Rhee wrinkling her nose from the strong mixture of spoiling milk and fruit. To her it did not look like anything could be saved from this wreck. The display cases—the shelves, the racks—cracked or split in pieces, were useless, and the only thing left intact, the large front counter, was scratched and covered with dents from heavy blows.

The police had wanted a description of some of the rioters, but Mrs. Rhee had seen nothing. She could describe a few of the boycotters, but she had been in the back room and had not seen anyone when they had come crashing through the front door. Mr. Rhee could do no better. He said everything happened too fast, that he had been too worried about the store and about their safety to have studied people's faces. It did not matter, thought Mrs. Rhee, since the police could not catch everyone who broke into the store. Mr. Rhee also said that Thomas had been outside when everything started to get violent, but neither of them knew where he had gone. On the ride in the back of the police car, Mrs. Rhee had seen the broken and vandalized stores, cars destroyed— one had been turned over and set on fire—and she wondered what had happened to Thomas. Had he been hurt, or had he run away?

She was still stunned by the damage in the store, and felt, above all, confused. Why had they done this to her? What purpose had this served? She could not understand it. She saw a small, brown rat run into a corner, and she jumped. Rats already. She found a broom and tried to poke the dark corners, hoping to drive it away. The rat shot across the floor and ran outside. They must clean this place as soon as possible. Where is the mop, she asked herself, looking at the mess. She heard Mr. Rhee sigh. He kicked aside some crushed boxes of cereal on the floor, and said in Korean, "Nothing is left here."

She did not reply, but stared at the different kinds of cereal that had spread out over that area—flakes, rice, loops, bright rainbow colors—and shook her head.

He leaned heavily against the wall, looking outside at nothing in particular. Then, after a long pause, he asked, "What happened to Thomas?"

She raised her head. "What?"

"Where is Thomas? Is he all right?"

Mrs. Rhee said, "He is the cause of this. It does not matter where he is."

"How can you say that?"

"How? He almost shot a customer! Because of that they boycott, and now this," she said. "He is the cause."

Mr. Rhee stared at her. "You know that this is not all his fault."

"You do not know what you are talking about!" she yelled. "Why are you always siding with him?"

Shaking his head, he said, "I do not know." He walked slowly into the back room.

Mrs. Rhee slammed the broom into the side of a broken shelf lying on the floor, and looked at the piles of garbage in front of her again. A police car drove by, its siren going off. Flashing lights entered the store for a second.

What were they going to do now? What about the other store, the expansion? They were not insured for this. She thought about Jung-Me's college fund, and she had to sit down. Everything was hitting her. What if they could not afford to send Jung-Me to college? She did not want to go into bankruptcy like the Kims had. That had been humiliating for them.

"No!" she said out loud.

Mr. Rhee looked out from the door.

She ignored him and began sweeping the food, the glass, and other debris into a pile at the center of the jagged aisle, the shelves knocked down at angles. No. She refused to accept that. They had too much to give up now. There was nothing else for them to do but push forward, no matter how hard it was. She found an empty box and began sweeping the garbage into it, occasionally pulling out a can or a package that seemed undamaged. Another police car sped by with its siren filling the streets.

After a half hour of cleaning, the store did not look much different. She had managed to clear one aisle, but that was all. Mr. Rhee went next door to use the phone. Mrs. Rhee was resting her legs and thinking about what to do next. So many things. What should they do with the broken shelves? They could not sell it. Will they have to throw all this away? Then, she saw Thomas walk in carefully, avoiding the pile of debris on the floor.

His shirt was dirty and ripped, and he was sweating, the sides of his face wet and dripping. Stains on his chest and underarms. He looked at her for a second, as if trying to recognize her, then said, "You're okay." He glanced at the floor. "I just wanted to check."

Check? She tried to keep her anger down. He acted as if nothing had happened! How dare he! Check? He did all this and he wanted to see it again? The store was gone, they might have to lose everything, and he pretended nothing was wrong!

"They said you were okay. Are you?"

Mrs. Rhee made a disgusted face, wrinkling her mouth and pointing around her. "Do we look okay?" she asked in English.

Thomas was surprised at her tone. He looked behind her. "Where is Mr. Rhee?"

"Mr. Rhee is not here," she said, raising her voice. "And you should not be here! You are the reason for this! You did this!"

He backed away, wide-eyed. "You don't know...."

"Don' know! Don' know! How—you!" She was so angry that the words were not coming out. This stupid, stupid *gyupo*, this...this.... She yelled, spitting and shaking, "Get out! You no work here!

Get out! No come back! Ever!"

He began to get angry, his body shaking, but he continued backing away.

"*Junum*! *Shang*!" She began yelling in Korean, unable to find the words in English. She called him stupid and lazy and he did not deserve to work anywhere, and they should never have hired him and she would make sure he never never worked with anyone she knew.

Mr. Rhee came running over. "Stop that!" he barked in Korean.

"He has the nerve to come here after what he has done! To come here and look at the ruin! At us!"

"Cursing him will not help anything!"

"Because of him we have nothing! Nothing at all! We are worse than when we first started! Nothing!"

Thomas turned around and ran out of the store, kicking the front door open which sent the remaining pieces of glass flying all over the sidewalk, and he kicked it again and again, and he turned and looked at Mrs. Rhee wildly, about to say something, but he kicked the door again and ran off, cursing, his breathing heavy and loud, wheezing.

Mr. and Mrs. Rhee stared at the empty doorway for a minute, and she began to calm down, knowing that she had lost her temper and she had to gain control, her heart still beating loudly, her hands sweaty. Her husband continued to stare out into the street, silent and angry. But she did not care. She could not believe that boy had come back. He had better not return again.

After a while, her husband said, "You did not have to do that."

"Yes I did. He deserved it."

"But he did not mean anything."

She shook her head, not listening. "He deserved it."

They returned to cleaning up, and did not speak to each other.

While Mrs. Rhee was examining the mess of cigarettes on the floor behind the counter, she heard three gun shots in a row, and she jumped. She and her husband glanced at each other. Two more shots followed. They went back to the cleaning and ignored it, Mrs. Rhee bending over, picking up the ripped cartons, tobacco, and crushed cigarettes spread all over the ground.

Δ

Goddamn her, he thought, running in a frenzy, shaking. Goddamn her store, her fucking screaming face didn't mean shit and blaming him for everything was stupid and plain fucking wrong since her goddamn racism was the cause of it and she didn't have to yell at him when he came by to help, so she could go fuck the store, the goddamn store. He was just so *sick* of everything and he had had it with them, the Rhees, with the damn boycotters, with everything and he couldn't stand it anymore, so he should just go, leave, die, and—where was he? Shit, walking in circles, in this mess, and he should go home, but he'd have to slip into side streets and alleys like a fucking thief though he wasn't the one stealing.

And you should not be here! You are the reason for this! You did this! Shut up, shut your fucking mouth, he screamed in his mind, thinking he wasn't the reason for that, and he didn't do that, goddamn it all, and he should have punched her in the fucking mouth that bitch—*she* was the one who started all this, *she* was the one who did this to him, to the store, to the fucking neighborhood! It wasn't his fault!

Ah, Christ, he thought, holding his head, the pain pulsing through his temples, into his forehead. Sweat dripped into his eyes, down his face, and he tasted the saltiness on his lips. Darkness fell onto the streets and everything wavered in his vision, nothing was solid, real, and he began walking faster, heading for what he thought was home. Home. Then what? Then you're alone again. Then you wake up to your own breathing, and go to sleep to your own heartbeat, and you're not working at that goddamn grocery anymore—what's going to happen to them now?—so you can find another job, away from here, away from everywhere. You can get money, hock a few things and then go somewhere else but where? Where would he go now—

What was that? Laughter. A familiar voice. In the alley, around the corner. Slow down, listen.

"You is k-killing this n-neighborhood." Very familiar...Mr. Harris? Yes, Mr. Harris...

"Shut the fuck up, old man." A young voice. An accent. "Where his wallet?"

"Here."

"G-Give that—" his voice cut off with a sharp breath. Look around the corner, slowly. Four Asian men surrounding Mr. Harris. The short muscular one with a crew cut holding him against the wall with his hand on Mr. Harris' chest, going through the pockets with the other hand. Mugging him!

"G-Go ahead. T-Take it, but you's never g-going to learn. You jus—"

"I said shut up." Hitting with an open hand against Mr. Harris' chest. Pain across his face. Assholes! Picking on an old man!

"This guy don't have nothing."

"Fucking great. Nigger, where your money? You got watch?"

"You ignorant kids—"

Hit him again, punching in his chest. "I

212

said shut the fuck up!"

Gun. Get the gun. Fucking assholes. Four to one. Punching him, four to one. Tough guys. Real tough guys to pick an old man. Sons of bitches. Chink sons of bitches.

"When you g-going to learn—"

"Shut up!" Punching him in the stomach, hard, and Mr. Harris doubling over, coughing, wheezing. Fucking four to one. Gun safety off. An old man.

Hey! Strange. Voice not sounding like you. Strangled-like. Gun shaking, keep steady.

Turning, surprised. Staring at the gun. Mr. Harris still coughing, holding his stomach. Spitting something. Blood? Blood! Assholes! What'd he ever do to them!

Let him go, you fucking shits. Picking on an old man, four to one.

One of them rolling his eyes. "Fucking A, put the piece away. What you think you doing?"

Let him go!

Waving the gun, letting them know you're not kidding. They push him away, Mr. Harris stumbling onto the sidewalk, doubled over in pain.

"Come on, what you do now?"

"Big man with gun."

Doesn't fucking matter anymore, nothing fucking matters, everything numb and these fucking *gang-peh* staring at you, one with a slight grin as if he thinks you're not serious, and you hate these men, these fucking cocky mean shits who pick on old men to rob and you see Mr. Harris leaning against the wall, trying to stand up, holding his stomach still coughing, splitting blood and the big Asian guy is smiling, fucking smiling, and probably thinking you can't even use the gun and what, he thinks you're a pussy a dumb chinko and this asshole's actually fucking smiling with a gun pointing in his face, *Think I'm fucking kidding do you? Think I'm fucking kidding you goddamn assholes!* and can't control anything, stop smiling, stop laughing, look at Mr. Harris, still coughing and you lower the gun to the man's bulging stomach and *Stop that fucking smile* with a fucking bullet and pull the trigger and the man's eyes widen for a fraction of a second as the hammer cocks back then slams forward and the gun explodes in your hand, kicking back, roaring in your ears, hurting your shoulder, and the fucking smile is gone, gone, and he falls forward, holding his stomach like Mr. Harris, and the man looks up in confusion and the other men are surprised but before they could do anything you turn the gun on another man, arm still smarting from the first one, and fire again, the gun kicking back harder, ringing in your ears, humming, the smell of gun powder and fire in your nose and your hand hot and burnt and the blood on the man's chest, *Stop that fucking* smile with fucking this, and then the next one don't stop and pull the trigger and the gun explodes again, hitting him in his throat and the red spurts out, *Stop that* fucking smile, and the blood reminds you of that time with June in bed and her blood all over the place, and time to *Stop* that fucking smile from the last guy's face, but before you have a chance the man jumps away and pulls something out of his jacket and there are two explosions going off in your face, one, two, and a flash of light and pain all over, screaming, but nothing coming out, and dizzying voices, sounds, sirens, and it hurts everywhere and where are you and where was June, and every part of you screaming out and it hurts it hurts it hurts it

EPILOGUE

Tom can tell by the quiet, and by the coolness in the air that it is late in the night. Nurses walk by less frequently, television sounds are off, and the voices, the murmurs, the background noise of this ward has stopped. He is alone. He remembers nothing right after that evening with those men and the pain that flashed through his head and body, and he woke up enveloped in that whiteness he had dreamed about, a whiteness that stayed around him for what seemed like forever, an ever-lasting blinding coldness like a cruel sun, and though this reminded him of his nightmares, he was not in pain, nor was he struggling in the midst of this. He was calm. He was quiet. Noises floated around him— voices, coughs, footsteps, a radio in the distance, whispers—and he was not sure where he was, since he could not see, and the noises around him were bodiless, formless, with swirling origins first in front of him, then behind him, then to one side and to the other. Dizzying. He wanted to ask someone where he was, but he could not speak, the breath unable to force any words out—it was as if he were no longer connected, and he faded in and out of this state, coming in to voices with such clarity that the words branded his mind, and then moving away, everything so murky, so chaotic. ...*Can you hear me? If you can, squeeze your left hand....* Tom could hear him, but he could not squeeze his left hand, nor his right, nor move his toes, his mouth, his tongue...nothing, and he felt curiously detached ...*No response....* What is going on, he thought, fading away again, and the voices came from a small tunnel, echoing strangely in the distance, and he ignored them, glad to be free of the immobility and of the confusion, and he was back in the whiteness that was slowly being shaded with blues, and he thought, How interesting, this is familiar. The blues and whites mixing together, and the sound of the ocean nearby, the lulling waves repeating their rhythmic crashes in his mind—or maybe not in his mind—and the cries of seagulls hovering around him in the clear sky, gliding in the wind, rising and falling with each gust.

  He is at the beach with his mother, and he is young, maybe three or four, and it is a sunny, hot day with breezes coming in from the ocean, blowing up some of the cool sand under their rented red and yellow umbrella. He plays with his green plastic pail and shovel, digging up sand, filling the pail, then dumping it back out, a meaningless repetition that calms and comforts him as the sounds of the sea layer upon his concentration, and his mother is laughing, watching him and pointing to the pile of sand next to him, saying something like, You're so funny, and although he does not understand what she means or why she said that, it does not matter, since he likes it when she is happy, and he fills the pail again, and levels off the sand carefully with the shovel, and then in one quick motion turns it upside down and it falls out over his leg. He feels the silkiness cover his knee and watches it disappear in the soothing, moist sand. He looks up. There do not seem to be any others around—they have this beach, this ocean, all to themselves—and he digs his fingers and toes into the piles he has made, and he listens to his mother's laughter, and he feels happy. He is happy. ...*Can you hear me Tom? God, I'm not even sure it's you with all these things here....* He faded in and out, enough to hear a familiar but not so familiar voice and he could not quite make out who was talking and what was being said, and he did not know if he was imagining it since nothing seemed real anymore, but he no longer cared. Did anything matter? He faded in less and less and he liked it that way, the return to his body a sad departure from the sea. He thought about what the voice was trying to tell him, something about hanging on, but it was so difficult for him to listen, to hear, to concentrate, and he knew everything was all right now, that everyone was safe. He wondered what June was doing now, where she was, what she was thinking, and he missed her, but maybe it was better that he was alone, here, though where was here? Another familiar voice, so familiar, echoing in his mind, though he was not sure where it was coming from, maybe inside him, and he remembered hearing this voice a long time ago. *Come on now.* Who was that? ...*Come on big boy, time to change those sheets. Upadaisy. Whew, you gettin' light as nothing....* Where was he, why was everything so...quiet? Nothing to hear anymore? Nothing to listen to?

Δ

He remembers now. June visited him twice, and he recognized her voice but couldn't respond. He drifted in and out and didn't understand all that she was saying, news about her parents and the store and how she was so sorry all of this happened. Tentative footsteps approaching and leaving—he remembers that. Clearing of her throat. Long silences. They no longer have the store. Her mother is distraught.

Tom imagines her mother with June, and using what June told him, he sees this: Mrs. Rhee and June are watching the television news in the living room of their small Riverdale co-op. The news tells of a new Korean/African-American Alliance to deal with interracial conflicts in wake of the tensions in Kasdan. The damage and losses from the thefts and fires during that time is estimated to be as high as five million dollars, with the death toll at three, including one police officer. The Korean/African-American Alliance feels that this racially motivated uprising is indicative of a larger problem of inner city discontent and hopes to address these concerns.

Mrs. Rhee stands up and walks to the window, ignoring the report. Their apartment is sparse and simple, with a few Korean decorations sent over by Mrs. Rhee's sister in Seoul: a large folding partition against the wall, soft golden birds and bamboo shoots painted on the screen, *hanja* lettering going down the right side, telling of the *Jen*, or goodness, espoused by the Confucian Analects. An open fan hangs on the opposite wall, its blue and gold peacock feathered design sharply contrasting against the bare white wall.

They are on the twentieth floor of the south building in the Skyview Complex. They have a view of the dirty Hudson River, though right now only some cargo ships lit up inside and along the deck can be seen on the river. It is a soothing view at night, with little river traffic and the lights moving slowly down past the docks. After staring out the window for a while, Mrs. Rhee sits back down on the old torn sofa, her mind wandering as the news story goes over events that she has thought about hundreds of times the past couple of weeks, trying to find some hope in what seems like a situation without any. She has even seriously thought about returning to Korea, though she knows she cannot, with Jung-Me in her last year of high school and her sights on college. And they do not have money for that kind of extravagance, picking up and moving to Korea. She checks the clock on the wall.

"He said he'd be late," Jung-Me says, not taking her eyes off the television.

Mrs. Rhee nods. She is worried about her husband who is coming home tonight with the news of the bankruptcy proceedings. They can no longer keep either of the stores and even after they sell everything they have, there will still be thousands of dollars of debt. Her husband said that they might have to give up their co-op, live by a court-appointed budget, and work off what they owe.

Work as what? was all she could say. What else can they do? What else can she stand? She hates the idea of working at her in-laws' laundromat in New Jersey, their only choice at the moment. She thinks of Mr. Casey at his laundromat—how unhappy he seems and how hard his work is, being with dirty clothes all the time, steam and the smell of

machines. Cleaning other peoples' dirty clothes re-
pulses her. And her sister-in-law, a large bossy
woman who thinks she knows everything, would
make life awful. Mrs. Rhee knows that the woman
would love to order her around. They have never
liked each other.

She sees herself behind a steam press:
her face red and sweaty, her hands burning from
detergent and ironing. Her day would be spent in
front of the machine, pressing shirt after shirt, pants
after pants, and she would not see anyone except her
sister-in-law. It would be worse than working in a
rice field in the summer. Stories her father told her, of
snakes and leeches, are still vivid in her mind. At
least in a rice field she would have fresh air. At a
laundromat she would be trapped inside, the constant sound of machines making her deaf. Her life
would be miserable.

She tries not to worry about this, although this has been on her mind constantly since
they closed the New York store. That was a terrible
day, when they locked the gate for the last time. They
managed to salvage a few shelves, a display rack,
and the things from the back room. Then they turned
in their keys. After four hard years, this was all they
had—some pieces of junk—and they had to sell even
that. Had it been worth it? Why should she even
bother working hard if they would lose everything?

Maybe she should give up, and be like the Kims after they went bankrupt, Mrs. Kim working for minimum wage at a Korean restaurant, Mr. Kim a janitor at a health club. They had no money, but their jobs took nothing from them, only time. But the money—she could not stand being truly poor.

The news ends, and her daughter stands up. "Where are you going?" Mrs. Rhee asks in Korean.

"Nowhere," Jung-Me answers in English. She walks into the kitchen and opens the refrigerator.

Mrs. Rhee watches her, wondering how much her daughter knows about their situation now. Trying to protect her daughter from worrying about this, Mrs. Rhee told her only that they were closing the store, but everything will be fine. A lie. But she sees no reason to tell Jung-Me everything, even though Mrs. Rhee suspects her daughter knows most of it. Her daughter is smart. But she wants Jung-Me to concentrate on school, not on family problems. Jung-Me sits back down with a drink and they watch a game show together. Mrs. Rhee never liked these shows, but she sits still and watches the contestants try to answer hard questions.

"Did you finish your homework?" Mrs. Rhee asks.

"Yes."

They remain silent. Mrs. Rhee thinks her daughter is so quiet these days—she never goes out anymore. Maybe she is like her mother who is always feeling so tired. Never has she been so run-down from doing nothing. Maybe this is why she has to always do something, concentrate on something else, otherwise her body begins to wear down, and she becomes sad. She is getting old.

When Mrs. Rhee hears the door, she stands and goes to meet her husband. "What did the lawyer say?" she asks as soon as he comes in, trying to keep her voice down so Jung-Me will not overhear.

"*Aigoo*, it is as bad as we thought. We have to move, and work off the debt."

Mrs. Rhee's insides fall. Even the smallest hope of good news has died.

"And," he goes on, "every month a part of our income will be automatically taken away by the courts."

Like children they are treated. "So we will have to work in your brother's laundromat?"

He nods.

"And we move to New Jersey?"

He nods again. "We stay with them for a few months, until we can find something of our own."

"But they will know! They will know we have lost everything!" She can imagine their pitying stares, their false concern and the noble position they would feel they were in. She cannot stand this.

"Keep your voice down. Yes, they will know. Everyone will know. We have lost everything."

"What about Jung-Me?" she asks, her voice a whisper. "What do we tell her?"

"We tell her what happened. We tell her we are bankrupt."

Mrs. Rhee feels ashamed. They have to admit their failures to their own daughter. The humiliation of everyone knowing is made worse by her daughter knowing. What kind of example are they? What will their daughter think now—that working hard does not mean she will succeed? That everything can be taken away no matter how hard she tries?

No. If they did not succeed, it was only because they did not work hard enough. Her husband walks away, and leaves Mrs. Rhee alone near the front door. She stares at her daughter watching television, and wonders what Jung-Me's reaction will be. Will she be ashamed of them? But what else can they do?

"What's the matter?" her daughter asks in English. Mrs. Rhee realizes that she is standing in the doorway, just studying her daughter. Where is her husband? She hears him in the bedroom.

"Nothing. I am thinking," she answers

in Korean. Sometimes when she sees her daughter, she thinks of Thomas. She has no idea where he is now, or what he is doing, and she tries not to think of him with her daughter. No matter. He is gone for good. She has more important things to worry about. She knows that if they work hard enough, they will do well. But, will they? They worked so hard for the Fruit 'N Food, and now they have nothing. But what else can they do? What other choice do they have? Give up? Forget about Jung-Me and college? She feels a tightening grip around her throat as she walks into the bedroom to speak with her husband.

Δ

Tom finds it difficult to believe that the Fruit 'N Food has closed down and the Rhees are out of business. He realizes his working there was, really, meaningless, and though he had thought he might belong there, belong somewhere, he had been wrong. But there is somewhere he does belong, he realizes, and he wonders if the beach was a dream or if it really happened. There were many things he could have done differently, things he should have done to avoid what wasn't an inevitable conclusion of violence, but what does it matter now? He can't care anymore. He remembers the street preacher with the Bible and megaphone on Amber and Banks telling the city that the end was near, but everything is so unclear now. What were they supposed to do?

What did he tell them?

He doesn't care anymore. He doesn't care where he is, what has happened to the Rhees, what will happen to him. He finds himself in pain more and he resists being led up and away to different rooms, to places away from his bed which terrorize him, and he soon doesn't acknowledge anyone. He learns with every passing day how to shut everything out, until he becomes as inert as the day he arrived. He withdraws more into his world of dreams, and drifts longer and longer. He has nothing to come back to, and he ignores his counselor when she asks him to react to the world around him. What do you hear? What do you feel? He doesn't want the outside world to exist.

In the cool and quiet night, Tom begins drifting again. The sounds of the ocean are louder, stronger, and he wants so much to go into the water. He wants to feel the waves splashing over him, to feel the cold water push under him. He wants to float on his back, the water in his ears blocking out everything except the whispers of the currents; listen, listen to the whispers, and he fades away, ignoring the echoing voices and concentrating only on the sounds of the oceans and the gulls, and somehow he knows this is better, and there is no reason to go back, and he feels the hot sand under his feet, and he runs into the ocean, the icy blue foam engulfing him.

Leonard Chang was born in New York City, and raised on Long Island. He attended Dartmouth College, Harvard University, and the University of California at Irvine. He currently lives near San Francisco, and is at work on a new novel.